Love Me Even When It Hurts 2

Jelissa

Lock Down Publications and Ca$h
Presents

Love Me Even When It Hurts 2
A Novel by *Jelissa*

Jelissa

Lock Down Publications
P.O. Box 870494
Mesquite, Tx 75187

Visit our website @
www.lockdownpublications.com

Copyright 2018 Love Me Even When It Hurts 2

First Edition May 2019
Printed in the United States of America

This is a work of fiction. Names, characters, places, and incidents either are products of the author's imagination or are used fictitiously. Any similarity to actual events or locales or persons, living or dead, is entirely coincidental.

Lock Down Publications
Like our page on Facebook: Lock Down Publications @
www.facebook.com/lockdownpublications.ldp
Cover design and layout by: **Dynasty Cover Me**
Book interior design by: **Shawn Walker**
Edited by: **Lauren Burton**

Stay Connected with Us!

Text **LOCKDOWN** to 22828 to stay up-to-date with new
releases, sneak peaks, contests and more…
Or **CLICK HERE** to sign up.
Thank you.

Like our page on Facebook:

Lock Down Publications: Facebook

**Join Lock Down Publications/The New Era Reading
Group**

Visit our website @
www.lockdownpublications.com

Follow us on Instagram:

Lock Down Publications: Instagram

Email Us: We want to hear from you!

Submission Guideline.

Submit the first three chapters of your completed manuscript to ldpsubmissions@gmail.com, subject line: Your book's title. The manuscript must be in a .doc file and sent as an attachment. Document should be in Times New Roman, double spaced and in size 12 font. Also, provide your synopsis and full contact information. If sending multiple submissions, they must each be in a separate email.

Have a story but no way to send it electronically? You can still submit to LDP/Ca$h Presents. Send in the first three chapters, written or typed, of your completed manuscript to:

LDP: Submissions Dept
Po Box 870494
Mesquite, Tx 75187

DO NOT send original manuscript. Must be a duplicate.

Provide your synopsis and a cover letter containing your full contact information.

Thanks for considering LDP and Ca$h Presents.

Dedication

To the greatest man I know, I love you with everything that I am. I thank God for you, for the wonderful man you are. Your encouragement and desire to see me push further in my writing career has been my driving force. Thank you for seeing in me what every other man has failed to see. You've loved me at my worst and loved me at my best. I'm forever yours.

To my baby boys RayJ & AJ, Mommy loves you. Everything I do is for you two. Thank you for being the greatest sons ever! Mommy loves you with all her heart.

Jelissa

Chapter 1

Sharome "Rome" Mills

My eyes grew heavy from the overwhelming events of the days prior. No matter how hard I tried, they seemed to have had a mind of their own. It'd been nearly four days since I'd been able to get a halfway decent night's rest. My mind wouldn't allow my brain to calm down enough to shut itself down so I could reboot. So many new revelations about myself and my parents had my head spinning so fast I felt dizzy.

I lowered the sun visor to block the attack of sunlight threatening to give me a migraine. Pulling the latch on the seat, I reclined it back just enough to get comfortable, then closed my eyes. A'Leeseea had promised her visit with her father wouldn't go past three hours. I was going to try my best to get some form of rest while she was in there finding out all of the answers to the questions surrounding us.

I reached and turned on some nice jazz on the radio, then lay back and closed my eyes. Almost immediately the image of my mother's face appeared, framed by the Korean necktie that was placed around her throat before she bled out, murdered by a man who I'd recently found out was my own biological father. I shook my head and tried to think of other things, but there she was again, haunting me, forcing me to face the reality of my decision. I'd allowed her to die while Leesee, the love of my life, lived on safely beside me.

I felt myself shaking like crazy. The guilt from the situation started to eat at me worse than ever, and because of my decision to stand by Leesee, my brother, Kazi was hollering revenge, swearin' he was going to murder me and her in cold blood.

Jelissa

I sighed and turned on my side, praying my mind would stop wandering so deeply. I needed to rest. I felt myself becoming weaker and weaker every single moment. I yawned and covered my mouth as I squeezed my eyelids tighter.

I heard the sound of cars coming to a screeching halt beside me, first on my right side and then on my left. I snapped my eyes open wide as saucers just in time to see the men emptying out of the black van to my right with masks on their faces and assault rifles in their hands.

I dropped down to the floor of the driver's side and covered my head as the gunfire erupted.

Boom. Boom. Boom. Boom. Boom.

The glass shattered and spilled all over my body and into my ear canal, but the shots didn't stop coming. The windshield exploded and the driver's door was pulled open, and that's when things got real.

"We got a message from Kazi!" the masked gunman said before aiming his assault rifle right at me and pulling the trigger again and again.

I felt the first bullet enter into my shoulder, stinging at first before becoming the worst pain I'd ever felt in my life. Before I could get used to that feeling, his second bullet pierced the side of my head, knocking a chunk out of it. The third one found its way into my face, lodging itself in my sinuses. My body started to shake as more and more bullets filled me up.

The gunman kept on saying, "This message is from Kazi, cuz!" as he and his hittas pulled their triggers again and again until I faded to black.

***

A'Leeseea "Leesee" Evans

10

Love Me Even When It Hurts 2

Rah'nell pulled me into a tight embrace then took a step back, looking me over closely with a concerned look on his face. "Baby, what's the matter? You look so down."

I blinked tears. "I need you to tell me if you're really my father. And if you aren't, then who is? I'm so tired of everybody lying to me. I need the truth, and I need you to be the one to give it to me. Can you do that?" I asked, feeling like I was on the verge of breaking down.

He nodded his head, then took my hand and led me to my seat before sitting across from me. Once we were seated, he reached across the small table and grabbed my hand again, looking into my eyes. "Baby, what has happened? What's making you come all the way out here to ask me these questions all of the sudden? Did your mother put you up to this? Is this her way of trying to have you turn your back on me like she has?" he asked with his right eyebrow raised.

I yanked my hand away and shook my head in anger. "Look, Daddy, this ain't about her and you. It's about me. Now I need to know the truth because my mind is screwed up right now. I felt like you were the only person I could turn to who wouldn't lie to me if I asked you flat-out. I mean it's one thing to keep a secret, and it's another to lie straight to a person's face when you're asked a direct question. I don't think you'd do me like that, so please tell me the truth. Are you my father?"

He took a deep breath and leaned back in his seat, rubbing his big hands on his prison-issued gray pants. Then he reached down and picked a piece of lint off his Timbs. "Yo, I been ya father since day one, li'l mama. Ain't nothin' gon' ever change that, nah mean?"

I noticed he avoided any form of eye contact with me. That was my first clue he was hiding something. I felt myself getting really angry already, and I was trying so hard to keep my composure, but I was so tired of everybody playing around with my life as if it didn't mean anything. They acted as if I was nothin' more than their own form of property, and I was sick of it. I sat up in my seat and leaned my head backward, opening my eyes wide to keep the tears from falling out of them. I looked over at him even though he continued to avoid eye contact with me. "So, I guess you're going to bullshit me around, too, then? You gonna be like everybody else in my life? Just to use me in your own selfish way?" I shook my head. "This shit is so ridiculous."

He frowned and finally looked over to me. "Oh, so you cussing in front of me now and shit? When you start doing this?" he asked, sitting on the edge of his seat as if he was getting ready to jump out of it and attack me.

I slammed my hand on the table so loud he jumped a little. "Look, I didn't come all the way out here so you can jerk me around. Now I need some answers, and I ain't leaving until you give me some." I sat on the edge of my seat and leaned across the table, looking him in the eyes with anger. I didn't care that everybody in the small visiting room was looking at us now. I acted as if they weren't even there. "Are you my fucking father or not, Rah'nell? And I'm talking biologically, not none of that other crap."

The guard, some old white man with a bald head, walked over to our table with his hand next to his pepper spray and stood beside Rah'nell. "Hey, is there a problem over here, inmate Richards?" he asked, looking from Rah'nell to me.

He shook his head and curled his upper lip in disgust. "Nah, ain't no problem. Just hollering at my seed, man. You got a problem?"

They looked at each other for a moment without saying any words, then the white man grunted and turned, sucked his teeth loudly, looking from me to Rah'nell once again. "Well, we don't tolerate disturbances in this prison. I don't care who you're visiting. Keep the noise to a minimum or I'll have to terminate your visit. This is your last warning." He sucked his teeth loudly one more time, mugging Rah'nell before walking off and looking all around the visiting room, probably for somebody else to harass.

"Word is bond, I hate these muthafuckas. I shouldn't even be here, li'l ma, but it is what it is." He sat back in his seat and dusted his pants off again. "Yo, look, now you asking to know what's really good wit' everythang, so I'ma tell you, but you better be strong enough to handle this shit. 'Cause if you ain't, it's gon' kill me. That's on my mother."

I swallowed my spit and sat up straight. "You don't have any idea what all I've been through. I can handle anything you about to throw at me, long as it's the truth. I don't want you sugar-coating nothing. Can you do that?" I asked, looking him directly in the eyes. I wanted to see if he was gon' avoid any eye contact. That was his tell when he was getting ready to lie to me. I think deep down he didn't like lying to me.

He ran his tongue across his teeth, then nodded his head. "A'ight, go ahead. Ask me anything, and I'ma keep it one hunnit."

"Are you my biological father? Did you and my mother have sex and make me? Am I your flesh and blood? There, I covered all of my bases so you can't skate around this question."

He shook his head. "Nah, Leesee. I ain't. You my daughter no matter what, but nall, we ain't blood-related." He exhaled loudly and ran his hand over his deep waves. "What else you wanna know?"

So, it was true, he really wasn't my father. I felt a lump forming in my throat. For over eighteen years he had been the only father I had ever known. I felt like I'd been cut deeply. I was almost scared to ask my next question, but I knew I had to.

"Since you're not, then who is?"

He sighed loudly, lowered his head, then shook it. "That nigga Kaleb yo' daddy. He the only one your mother was messing wit' around that time on a daily basis. I mean, besides me. I can't even have kids ever since my car accident when I was little, but I always wanted a child. Yo' moms knew I couldn't have kids, but she wanted one just as bad as I did. I low-key gave her permission to fuck around wit' dude for the purpose of bringing you into this world. Now, back when she got pregnant with you, her and that li'l broad Shavon was beefing real bad from somethin' I'm not too sure about. I just remember them getting in a big fight, and her almost losing you. Anyway, about her fourth month, that nigga Shotgun set Kaleb up to get killed just to get him out of the way. He was obsessed with your mother, and I didn't even know it. Around that time, I'd gotten knocked for possession of heroin and an unlicensed firearm. They made me serve six months in the county jail. The whole time me and Deidre were tight, but she was fuckin' wit' Shotgun on the side, and I didn't know it. Before I'd gotten locked up, me and him was pretty tight. So, when I touched down, we hooked back up and he put me on my feet with a li'l weight. Long story short, after you were born that fool became psychotic over Deidre. We were out receiving a big shipment of heroin down in Trenton when Shotgun flipped out and asked to see my pistol, and I fucked wit' the homie, so I gave it to him. Man, why'd I do that? As soon as I did, he started shooting. He hit the plug, which turned out to be an undercover agent, and then he hit one of the niggaz we were with and popped himself in the shoulder and blamed that shit on me. I was devastated. That nigga did all this shit for your mother."

I bugged my eyes out of my head and held my face. I couldn't believe what I was hearing. I felt like scabs were being taken off of my eyes.

"What other questions you got? Let's get all this shit out in the open right now so we can leave it in the past."

"Is Nia really his daughter? Like, do you really know for a fact?" It really wasn't that important, but I just wanted to know.

He nodded. "Hell yeah. That li'l girl look just like Shotgun. He can't deny her. Deidre told me that Nia's brother stay right next door to y'all, and so do yours. But I don't think Shavon told them what's good," he laughed. "You gon' have

14

to do that." He adjusted himself in his seat. "How that fool been treating you? I know he been spoiling you and everythang, huh?"

I covered my face with my hands and exhaled loudly. "He been fucking me since I was a little girl. Now he trying to hunt me down so he can kill me." I blurted the words out so fast it was too late to assess what I was saying. I had promised myself before I came that I wasn't going to tell him all of that.

"What?" He stood up with a mug on his face, and the old guard from before made eye contact with him. He sat down and reached across the table, grabbing my hand. "Princess, what do you mean?"

I blinked and tears ran down my cheeks. "Shotgun thinks he owns me. He calls me his baby girl and says he's the only one who can have me. He forces me to call him daddy, and I think he did somethin' to my mother and Nia because I haven't heard from either of them in over a week, and I found blood on the rug in our house. I'm scared out of my mind."

He closed his eyes and shook his head. "Damn. What, that nigga ain't been taking his meds or somethin'? Do Deidre know he been going in on you like that?" He looked hurt.

I shrugged my shoulders. "Yeah, I'm pretty sure she does, but she doesn't care about me no more. The only person I got is Sharome. He been holding me down through all of this, even chose to save my life over Shavon's. Oh yeah, Shotgun kilt her, too. That dude on a rampage, which is why I'm so worried about my mother and Nia." I felt my stomach rumble and a sudden wave of dizziness came over me. "Are you hungry? You want me to get you something from the machines?"

He waved the idea off. "Under normal circumstances, maybe, but right now I'm worried about you. You know Sharome is his son, right? he may not know it, but Shotgun do. It's probably driving him crazy knowing y'all messing around. He didn't even like Shavon breast feeding li'l dawg 'cause it made him jealous. I can only imagine what's going

15

through his crazy-ass brain right now," he scoffed. "Yo, you definitely ain't safe wit' that nigga on the lose. Y'all gotta get out of Jersey fast or he gon' have you killed. Any type of phones or cars he bought, get rid of that shit, because he gon' track you down by it nine times out of ten. I got a few plugs in Harlem I'ma hit up out of love for you as soon as I get back on the unit. Once everything is good, I'ma send you an email. Make sure you get rid of that phone you got right away. I'm telling you, it's dangerous." He sat on the tip of his chair and stroked my hand. "Look, I don't know what you goin' through out there, but I just wanna let you know I love you, and as far as I'm concerned, you'll always be my daughter. I'm sorry for failin' you and allowin' this nigga to strip me away from you. Had I been there, I would've rather met death than let you be harmed. You're my princess, no matter if my blood is running through your veins or not. You live in my heart, and that will never change."

After he left, I went into the visitors' bathroom and cried my eyes out. I was so lost and so hurt. I couldn't believe the truths I'd found out. I didn't know which way to go, but once again I found myself praying Sharome stayed by my side and never left me. I needed him more than ever now. I knew we were in this crazy life together, and one day we'd probably die beside one another. And as crazy as it sounded, as long as I was dying beside him, I was ready to meet death.

16

Chapter 2

Rome

Boom. Boom. Boom. Boom.

The shots got louder and louder, and then a gust of cold wind hit my face. The bright lights from the gunshots were blinding me. I felt the masked gunman place the barrel of his gun to my chest and pull the trigger again before taking his mask off to reveal his identity. Kazi curled his upper lip and smiled real evil.

"Sharome! Sharome! Sharome!"

Boom. Boom. Boom. Boom.

"Sharome!"

More blood poured from my forehead and ran down my neck.

"Sharome! Sharome! Fuck!"

I snapped open my eyes as the sound of gunfire faded away. I jerked in my seat, feeling all over my body for blood and the bullet wounds caused by Kazi and his men, but there were none.

Knock, knock, knock. "Sharome, open the door! Damn, you been in there sleeping like a bear," Leesee hollered from outside the Navigator.

I jerked up and popped the locks, wiping the sweat from my forehead and neck. The sun was cooking me alive. My entire shirt was drenched. "Damn, I'm sorry, baby. I must've dozed off. I was tired as hell."

She opened the passenger's door and got in. "It's good, but let's get the hell out of here. Oh, wait a minute." She opened the door all the way and got out, jumped into the air, and smashed her phone against the concrete before getting back into the truck and slamming the door. She placed her seatbelt around her and adjusted the air conditioner.

Jelissa

"So, how is your old man doing?" I asked, really not knowing what to say to her. She looked real down, and I was worrying he'd told her Shotgun was also her father. I didn't know what I would do if that was the case.

She shrugged her shoulders. "He's not my father, and neither is Shotgun. Kaleb was." She swallowed and looked out of her window. "I'm hungry. Let's pick up some barbecue before we head back to the hotel." She leaned forward and switched the tunes to a song by Jhene Aiko.

"Are you okay, baby? Is there somethin' you want to talk about?" I looked over at her as she continued to stare out her window in silence. I wondered what was going on in her mind and prayed that whatever she'd found out wasn't secretly hurting her more than she could handle. I didn't like to imagine her in pain. I loved her too much. I felt like I wanted to endure all of her pain for her. I wanted to cry her tears, so she didn't have to. All I wanted to do was protect her and keep her happy as much as possible. I needed her to be okay just so I could be. That was important.

She sighed and smiled. "Yeah, I wanna talk about everything he told me, but I'd rather do it once we get some food in us. I'm kinda dizzy, and I feel a migraine coming on. I need to calm down a little bit and just put everything into perspective. I know we have a bumpy road ahead of us, but I know together we can survive it." She reached over and placed her hand within mine, then interlocked our fingers.

Tia, Leesee's cousin, jumped out of the bed as soon as I slid the key card into the door and pushed it open. She looked like she was ready to jump under the bed in fear, obviously still in shock from all of the drama that had taken place at Marcy Projects, where two of her friends had been gunned down while rolling in Leesee's Jeep. We still weren't sure if the hit was meant to be for us or for Pappy, who was one of the people who had been killed. All I knew was me and Leesee were up against two cold-hearted individuals who wanted us

18

dead. Both had different forms of power, and neither would stop until we were lying in caskets. At least that's how I felt.

"Yo, y'all been gone all day. I been in here going nuts thinking somethin' done happened to one of you," she said, looking from Leesee to me.

Tia was about five-feet, three-inches tall and dark skinned with a gorgeous body. She owned two beauty salons in Brooklyn and worked as a topnotch feature stripper up and down the east coast. Far as I could tell, she was about her paper.

Leesee took her Prada leather off and tossed it on the bed before sitting down next to it, untying the laces of her Charles Davids. Then she kicked them off, scooted all the way to the headboard, and placed her back up against it. "Well, as you can see, we're good. You need to calm down, everybody is already freaked out enough." She looked up to me. "Sharome, bring them two trays over here and fill them up with the barbecue. I'm ready to get my eat on, then I need to get some rest, fo' real." She reached over to the night table and grabbed a bottle of hand sanitizer, squirting a portion in her palm before handing it to Tia. "Huh, you need to put some food in yo' ass, too."

Tia took the bottle and squirted some of it into her hand. "Yo, I been all over my Facebook, and everybody telling me it's been niggaz going all over the projects asking about me and y'all. They even offering up cash for our whereabouts. I don't know what the fuck y'all done got me into, but somebody betta tell me something because my life dependin' on it." She frowned and sat on the side of the bed after grabbing one of the trays from me and opening the platter of baby back ribs I was about to murder.

It took us ten minutes to get the food set up so everybody could reach it without spilling the sauce all over the blanket covering the bed. I was kneeling along the side of the bed, stuffing my face. I didn't know I was starving until I took that first bite of my ribs. Once that meat and special barbecue sauce hit my tongue, it was over. I was chewing with my eyes closed and everything. My fingers were full of sauce, and so were theirs.

Tia forked up a nice amount of Spaghetti and put it into her mouth. "So, y'all gon' let me know what's good, or what?" she asked, talking with her mouth full.

I broke a rib apart and got to digging out the meat before popping it into my mouth. I had eaten about six of them, and I was still hungry. "Tia. I'ma let yo' cousin holla at you, 'cause I don't know how much she want you to know. That ain't my bidness." I dumped some macaroni and cheese onto my plate and was already imagining how good it was going to taste.

Leesee shook her head and sucked her fingers at the same time, loudly. "Look, you already knew Shotgun was crazy as hell. That fool became obsessed with me, and after I left the crib and became involved with Sharome, he went ballistic. Now that nigga acting like he wanna kill both of our ass, and knowing him, sooner or later he probably will. I think he had somethin' to do wit' my Jeep getting shot up. If not him, then Kazi, because that nigga at us, too. They trying to break us apart, but ain't shit moving. That's my baby, right there. It's gon' take an army to pull us apart, and then some. Ain't that right, baby?"

I smiled. "You damn right. This here is to the death." I bit into another rib and closed my eyes. Damn, that shit was fire.

Tia stood up and arched her eyebrow. "Uh, so what that shit got to do wit' me? I mind my own bidness. Ain't no reason for them to be trying to kill me and shit. My friend Ke-Ke inboxed me sayin' one of the Crips ran up on her and said when he catches me, he gon' put one in my dome for hidin' their fugitives. I didn't even know what that meant until y'all just told me this shit." She started to pace the floor, and I kept right on eating. I had so many bones on my plate it looked like I'd devoured a whole-ass dinosaur.

Love Me Even When It Hurts 2

Leesee got out of the bed and walked toward the bathroom. "Don't even worry about it. We'll clear all that stuff up for you and let them know you ain't know what was good. Just chill."

Tia stopped mid-pace and scrunched her face. "Just chill? Just chill? Really? You gon' say some shit like that to me after two of my best friends just got murdered because the hittas thought they were y'all? Now they runnin' around the projects sayin' I'm the enemy, too. Fuck that, y'all don't know how them Crips is in Brooklyn. They ain't got no fucking hearts, and they'll kill a bitch just as quick as they would a nigga. They know where my shops at, know what clubs I work. Ain't no way I can chill. How the fuck am I gon' eat? Where do I go now? The projects are my whole-ass life. Always has been." She plopped down on the bed and lowered her head.

Leesee stopped in the bathroom door and shook her head. "We got you, girl, just let us figure some shit out. You gon' be good, though. I promise you that." She walked into the bathroom and closed the door.

I tossed all of my garbage into the black plastic bag, along with everybody else's, then started scrubbing my hands with the moist towelettes.

Tia stood back up and started to pace the floor again. "If it's niggaz looking for us in Brooklyn, we gon' have to get up out of there. I got a crib out in Harlem. I know a few good brothas out there. You trying to get yo' feet dirty with that work you got, it'll be the best spot to do it 'cause a whole bunch of the niggaz that used to hustle around there got indicted about a month ago, which means that territory is open. Plus, it's been a drought. Fein's been traveling all the way to Queens just to get some good dope. We set up shop on 113th and that money gon' come in by the barrels. Trust me on that."

I sucked at my teeth. "I'm down for whatever. If you sayin' it's good, we can move out that way tomorrow. My only question to you is how do you know them niggaz just gon' let me come hustle over there when I ain't never stepped foot in Harlem before?"

She waved me off. "My sister baby daddy hustle a li'l bit over there. His name Ralphie. them niggaz respect him. Long as y'all come to some form of an understanding, it'll be good. Just let me holler at him tonight, and we can make our way over there in the morning.

Later that night, around twelve in the a.m., Leesee got out of the bed where she'd been laying on my chest and walked out to the hotel's balcony, attempting to close the door behind her, but I caught it and followed her outside, handing her a coat and neglecting to put mine on myself.

"Here you go, baby. And what's the matter?" I placed her coat around her shoulders as she looked out into the night with her back to me. I stepped forward and slid my arms around her, placing my chin in the crux of her neck before kissing it and sucking all over her thick vein there.

"Mm, baby, that feels so good. I needed to feel that. My body calling for you like crazy, and I don't know what to do about it." She took a step backward and made her round ass press against my front. It felt glorious. I rubbed her li'l hips and sucked on her neck again, trailing my hands up to her stomach and rubbing upward until I was cupping her breasts. Somehow, she'd managed to take her bra off, so her globes were free, and I was loving 'em.

"I'm fien'ing for you, too, baby. I know we got a lot going on, but that ain't stopped me from craving you. You drivin' me nuts right now." I sucked her neck loudly, then licked into her ear, twirling my tongue around inside it.

"Uh. Shit." She turned around to face me and stood on her tippy-toes to trap my lips with her own.

The winter air blew against our bodies, but we seemed to pay it no mind. All that mattered to me was her heat and the scent coming from her. This woman had me nuts over her already, and I wanted some of her so freakin' bad.

Love Me Even When It Hurts 2

She ran her hands under my polo and rubbed my abs, then upward to my chest. "All these damn muscles. Damn, why my cousin gotta be here? I need you tonight, Sharome. With all this stuff going through my head, I just need to escape it all right now."

I picked her up and sat her on the railing, causing her to yelp. She opened her legs and I walked in between them, leaning forward and kissing her passionately while she wrapped her ankles around my lower back. "What you wanna do, baby? I'm down for whatever you wanna do. But let's do somethin'. Please," I begged. I felt like I was about to pass out from needing her so bad.

She looked over my shoulder and back into the hotel room where Tia was sleeping. She bit into her lower lip and moaned. "What if she catches us?"

I shrugged my shoulders. "Once again, I don't care, baby. I just wanna taste you. I need some part of you on my tongue. I'll be cool wit' that. Please." I attacked her neck and sucked it with force, all the while rolling her nipples with my thumbs and forefingers.

"Mm. Sharome." She moaned and humped into me. She looked over my shoulder and bit into her bottom lip.

"Let me taste you, Leesee. Please, baby. Let me taste you out here right now. That's all I ask. I'm begging you." I licked her neck and cupped her breasts together, wishing I could feel them on my lips. I was harder than a brick wall, yearning for her essence. I felt like I needed it.

She hopped off the railing and stood before me. "Okay, baby, you can taste me, but we gotta hurry up. I don't want Tia to catch us." She started to unbutton her pants.

I squatted down and took her pants and panties right along with me, bringing them to her ankles before turning her around so her round, brown ass was facing me. She leaned all the way over and spread her legs, and before she could get them all the way open my face was in her crease, licking up and down and sniffing that kitty up. When her juices invaded my tongue, I felt like I was about to cum from that alone. I opened her lips so I could get at her better. I wanted to drink her nectar as if it was wine or somethin'.

"Mm, Sharome. Uh! Baby. Mm, ah. It feels so good." She opened her ass cheeks further for me, reaching under herself and spreading her own sex lips apart, exposing her thick clitoris that stood erect and glistened with her juices. Her scent went up my nose and further encouraged me to go in even harder. "Yes, baby. Yes. Yes. Ooh, it feels so good."

I squeezed her booty with both hands and stuck my face as far into her as it would go, licking up and down, trapping her clit with my lips, sucking it like a third nipple.

"Mm. Mm. Smack my ass while you do it, baby, please. Ooh! Please, baby. I need you to." She opened her legs further and arched her back, pressing backward into my face even more.

Smack! I hit that ass hard twice, once on each side, and really got to eating that kat like I was starving. Licking up and down her slit, nipping at her clit with my teeth, then right back to sucking on her vagina's nipple with force.

She stood on her tippy-toes, then came off of them and backed into my mouth. "Uh! Uh! Sharome! I'm cumming! I'm cumming, baby. Ooh, smack my ass again! Smack it harder. Tear it up! Uh!"

And that's just what I did. I started attacking it while eating her for all she was worth while she screamed out loud and came all over my lips and mouth. I slurped up everything I could and swallowed her treasures.

She dropped down and pulled my dick out of my pants, stroking it up and down while looking me in the eyes and kissing all over the head. "I got you, too, baby. Just as bad as you need me, I need you the same way."

She pulled my skin backward, then sucked me into her mouth and got to running her hot lips up and down it. Her jaws hollowed out, and the loud sounds of her sucking had me on the verge. I could still taste her kitty on my tongue, and that was getting me, as well.

"Mm. Yeah, Leesee. Yes, baby. Do that." I groaned as I held the railing, looking down on her. I couldn't believe a female so bad was sucking me up like she was. It was turning me on so much I was having a hard time lasting. Well, that and the fact it was the first time I had ever gotten head before. In fact, I was a virgin altogether, but I didn't think Leesee knew that.

She speared her head in my lap again and again. I started to shake. There was a feeling in me I had never felt before, shooting all over my body. I felt happy, excited, and very weak all at the same time. The heat from her mouth intensified the feeling. The last thing I remembered before I started shooting was having visions of killing a muthafucka over her and lifting a veil off her face at our wedding. I groaned out and fell against her while she kept on sucking me like crazy. If I hadn't been in love with her before then, I definitely was now. I felt emotional as hell over this woman.

"Damn, y'all ain't have to come all the way out here to get it on. Y'all could have asked me to chill in the lobby for an hour or so," Tia interrupted as Leesee stroked my penis up and down in the cool night's air.

At hearing her voice, we started to get ourselves together. I didn't know how she was able to creep up on us. I thought Leesee was watching out for her, but obviously she got caught slipping.

"Ain't no sense in y'all trying to rush and get dressed. I done already seen everything he got, and you too, Leesee." She laughed and walked back into the hotel.

Leesee stood up, and I kissed all over her juicy lips, wrapping her into my arms and holding her as close to me as possible. I don't know why, but after our oral thing I was feeling her ten times more. Like she'd awakened somethin' in me I didn't even know was there.

She hugged me and lay her head on my chest. "I love you, baby. I mean that with all of my heart. Please never leave me, no matter what we gotta go through or who we're up against. Just never leave my side."

I moved her curly hair out of her face and looked into her eyes while I held her soft cheeks in my hands. "Baby, listen to me. I love you with all of my heart, and we are in this life together until our last breath. I'm about to make it happen for you. I just wanna give you the world until I get taken off of this muthafucka. I just need you to trust me and know I got us. I ain't gon' fail you. You're all I have and all I need in this world. Please believe that."

She nodded her head and smiled, both dimples appearing on her brown cheeks. "I do believe you, baby. I believe and love you with all of my heart. I'll die for you. I swear to the heavens I will."

Chapter 3

Idris "Shotgun" Wright

"That's three hundred thousand right there, cash money," I said, taking the last bundle of cash out of the money-counting machine and placing it into the Louis Vuitton suitcase beside me. "Gotta be one of the best licks we hit all year, baby. One-fifty to you and one-fifty to me. I already got that shit separated. Where you at with the heroin? How many bricks apiece?" I asked Hunter, my partner, as he wrapped the tan rope around his arm and tied it into a knot.

Hunter licked his lips and sniffed loudly. "Thirty kilos. That's fifteen apiece. If you wanna go in wit' me, I have a few Bloodz out of D.C. that's looking to cop at fifteen apiece. I know it's low, but we'll get ninety grand on the rebound. You know, once everything is sold. Those boys run a solid operation up there, and they aren't even on the FBI's watch list as of yet, so it's guaranteed money. I say we'll see a return in three months. That'll be forty-five grand apiece in June, what'll you say?" He took the tablespoon and scooped a nice portion of heroin into it, squeezed water out of the dropper into the spoon, then placed a fire underneath it, cooking the dope right before my eyes. After it started to bubble, he took his syringe and drew the poison into its body, licking his dry lips.

I wiped my mouth with my hand. "No dice. I'ma take my cut and do my own thing. You got that monkey on yo' back, too. Tough for me to take that risk. I can't stand any missteps right now." I shook my head and placed his hunnit and fifty gees on the table before pushing it across to him.

I watched him shoot the dope into his veins. His eyes rolling into the back of his head. "Mm, that's the stuff," he growled and clenched his teeth.

Jelissa

The money and heroin were the spoils from the Haitian Mafia we'd knocked off only earlier that same day. One of my confidential informants had given me the information on a drop that would prove to be quite lucrative. We intercepted a shipment of grade-A heroin that came from Don Sycleff and was supposed to be dropped at the warehouse of the Haitian mafia that had recently navigated to Newark, New Jersey from Miami. We'd hit the Mafia for the money, and Don Sycleff's cronies for the heroin. I was sure there was going to be a lot of backlash from the double crossings, but I didn't give a fuck. I was the police, and I was sure I could stay one step ahead. I had CI's within both of their organizations, and I kept them well fed. One hand washed the other.

Hunter got ready to shoot up another batch of dope.

"Say, Hunter, slide my kilos across the table, white boy, before you do 'em all." I looked him over with disgust.

He frowned and scooted his chair backward from the round table. "Got damn, Shotgun. You're a fucking buzz kill if I ever saw one. There's no fuckin' way I can do thirty kilos, man. It's just impossible." He reached into his suitcase and started to hand me two bricks at a time.

I grunted. "I know it's impossible to do thirty because fifteen of them is mine, and I'd be a damn fool if I sat here and let you fuck off my dope and yours." I took my bricks and placed them in my suitcase before zipping it closed.

Hunter sat back up and got to working on his next fix. "Those fuckin' Haitians aren't going to take this shit lying down, I hope you know this. That Don Sycleff is a sadistic muthafucka. The boys down in Miami say he's not one to be fucked with, and unfortunately for us we got the memo way too late, so we're up for it." He laughed. "We already have you running around town chasing the monkey that's on your back. Wonder how long that's gonna last?" He scooped up a spoonful of heroin and went back to getting it ready to shoot.

I rolled my head around on my neck. It had been two months since I'd seen my baby girl, my Leesee, and I was

Love Me Even When It Hurts 2

jonesing for her so bad I'd taken to fucking every bitch that shared her likeness, and most times I took them by force because it made it that much better. It was like a quick fix that only lasted for a few hours before I was fien'ing and lookin' for my next one. I mugged Hunter with hatred. "Well, I guess we all have our demons. As far as Sycleff goes, this is Jersey, not Miami, so fuck him. We got bigger fish to fry, and I got a lick that's double the size of this one that's going down in a few weeks for now we need to lay low, so I'll be in touch." I watched him inject the poison into his veins once again before nodding. I let myself out of his back door and jumped into my black-on-black Charger, heading toward my fix.

An hour later Simone, a Madame who specialized in sex trafficking, lead me into one of the luxurious rooms on the back of her mansion with a smile on her beautiful face. I watched her sway from side-to-side as she walked in front of me, sporting a silk gown that was so short that with every step she took it showed off the bottom halves of her brown ass cheeks. I had to give her props. Her body was immaculate, nice and athletic-looking, and she had to be every bit of fifty-plus years old.

She sipped white wine out of a wine glass with her pinky out. "I think you're going to like this one, Shotgun. She's nearly everything you asked for, and the kicker is with this one you can do whatever you want to her. Within reason, I mean. You can't kill her or nothin' crazy like that, but anything short of it is cool." She continued to lead the way. "I see you brought your little black bag. Got some things in mind?" she smiled, looking back over her shoulder at me.

I grunted. "Long as I'm paying you a thousand dollars to do whatever it is I want to do with the prospect you're placing in front of me, you don't worry about what I have in mind. It's personal," I said, a little more chippy than I meant to. I just didn't like her prying all into my bitness. We weren't cool, and I didn't want her to get too comfortable with me. This was

29

Jelissa

a business arrangement and nothin' more. I preferred to keep it that way.

She shrugged her right shoulder and closed her eyes, briefly looking back at me. "Excuse me for making conversation. Geez." She stepped to the last door in the long hallway and knocked on it twice before turning the knob and peeking her head inside of the room. Ten seconds later she opened the door all the way up and waved her hand, signaling me to step inside, which I did. "I'll be back in an hour," she said, stepping out of the room and closing the door behind her.

I looked across the bedroom and saw the pretty woman sitting on the bed, looking over at me as if she were almost shy for us to be alone together. As soon as we made eye contact, she lowered her head and hunched her shoulders inward. I made my way across the room until I was standing directly in front of her, taking her chin and lifting it upward so I could peer into her face now that I was closer.

"Uh! What are you doing?" she yelped as I took hold of her chin.

"Shut up, bitch, and just let me look at you. I gotta make sure you look exactly like my baby girl or I ain't laying a hand on you, and I'm going to get my money back," I said, pulling her arm so she could stand up, then I looked her over from head to toe. The first thing I noted was the mole on the right side of her cheek, just like Leesee's. She was the same caramel complexion. Her hair was also curly, just a few inches shorter than Leesee's was the last time I saw it. I made her turn in a circle, admiring her frame and feeling my penis harden in my pants. Her waist was small, like my baby's. Her ass poked out just enough to entice any man. She stood on bowed legs. Her toes were painted pink, just like I'd requested.

I turned her back around so she could face me and looked into her brown eyes, brushing her hair away from her face. "I've missed you, baby girl. Tell Daddy, have you missed him?" I asked, sniffing her scalp with my eyes closed now.

Love Me Even When It Hurts 2

Her long pause made me snap my eyes open and mug her with anger. She'd started to bite on her bottom lip nervously. "Uh, yeah, Dad. I've missed you a lot. What do you want to do today?"

I felt my blood boiling, and suddenly the room started to go hazy. I felt myself beginning to shake as I imagined Leesee standing there in front of me. I needed her so bad. I reached and grabbed her by her throat, slamming her into the wall before sucking on her neck and pulling up her tight skirt, sliding my hand into her panties. As soon as I felt her warm sex lips, I moaned out loud. "Mm, baby girl. Daddy been missing you so much. Why did you have to leave me? Don't you know how crazy I am over you?" I bit into her neck so hard it broke the skin before I was sucking again, pushing two fingers into her womb. I needed her body more than ever.

"Uh, wait a minute. We have to discuss the rules before we go this far," she screamed, trying to pull my hand out of her panties.

She looked scared and ready to panic, and it turned me on like crazy. There was nothin' like the feelings of scaring the shit out of a woman right before you dominated her ass. I picked her up and tossed her on the bed, straddling her waist, and ripping her clothes away. "I make the rules. I'm yo' daddy. You do what the fuck I say, and I say I want this body, and I want it right now. You're my baby girl!" I ripped her panties off of her frame and sniffed the crotch, turning them around and licking up and down it, before tossing them over my shoulder. I ripped her blouse off her and tore her bra causing her titties to spill out. I grabbed them and squeezed them together, sucking all over the huge, brown nipples that stood at attention.

She constantly squirmed under me. "Wait a minute. Get off of me, please. I need to see Simone. I need to tell her I'm not okay with this. I thought we were just going to – argh!"

I grabbed a handful of her hair and pulled her halfway off the bed so I could dig the handcuffs out of my bag that I'd

31

placed on the table beside the bed. I pulled out two pairs and handcuffed her wrists to the headboard while she squirmed under me.

"Hey, wait a minute. I need to holler at Simone. I don't want to do this. I'm scared," she whimpered loudly.

I sucked down her body, stopping right between her breasts, taking them and squeezing them together with my eyes closed. "Mm, Leesee. I missed this, baby. I missed the feel of my baby girl's soft body." I leaned down and sucked on her nipples roughly before pulling on them and wiggling out of my pants, sucking further down her body until I got to her pussy. I stuck my nose right in the center of her sex lips and inhaling as hard as I could. It gave me shivers. My dick was sticking out of my boxers. "I gotta fuck you now, baby. Daddy gotta have some of his baby girl right now. I can't take it anymore!" I growled, sliding out of my boxers and running my dick head up and down her wet crease.

She wiggled her hips from right to left, trying to shake me off of her. "No, you have to use a condom. I'm not doing this unless we use protection. Please, sir."

I leaned down and bit into her left thigh so hard my teeth came together in her skin, and she screamed out loud and tried to break out of the handcuffs. Then I sat up and choked her with my right hand and forced myself between her thick thighs. "Bitch, you belong to me. You're my muthafuckin' baby girl, and I hit this pussy however I want to. You understand me? Nod yo' fucking head!" I hollered through clenched teeth, applying pressure to her throat.

She nodded, and her eyes got as big as saucers as I slammed into her gushy pussy and got to fucking her with all of my might. Long, hard strokes sank to her bottom again and again. I would choke her for nearly a full minute, allow her to breathe, then choke her all over again. In my mind's eye she was Leesee, my li'l girl who had abandoned me for my own son. I loved her and hated her all at the same time. She made me weak and sick. I needed to find her, and I was doing everything I could to do just that.

I fucked that girl for forty-five ·minutes straight with no mercy. My eyes closed tight, seeing the face of my obsession. I needed her, and I had to have the real Leesee real soon, and there was nothing or no one going to stop me from tracking my baby down.

After I climbed from between her legs and un-cuffed her from the headboard, she nearly tackled me to the bed and sucked my limp dick into her mouth. "Mm. Oh my god. Ain't nobody ever fucked me like that. It felt so good, mister. Please tell me you'll be back. I'll be your little girl. I'll be your Leesee. Just say you'll be back," she begged and sucked me off and on at the same time.

I pushed on her forehead and made her fall backward after yelping. "What's you name, li'l girl?" I asked, standing up and sliding into my boxers. I was winded, and my dick felt sore as hell.

She lay on her back and opened her thick thighs wide, rubbing her still very wet pussy, sliding two slim fingers deep into her middle, pulling them in and out with her eyes lowered. "My name is Tracy, but it can be whatever you want it to be."

I laughed at that. "And how old are you?" I slipped into my shirt and tucked it into my pants, taking the handcuffs and placing them back inside my black party bag.

"Well, Simone says I'm eighteen, so I'm eighteen. Everything else doesn't matter. So, when can I see you again?" she asked, rubbing her stomach and licking her lips.

I didn't know how, but she was turning me on all over again. She looked so much like Leesee that I was having a hard time. "How long you been working for Simone?" I needed to know how many miles she had on that pussy. It felt tight and fresh, so I knew she couldn't have been working that long. Nall, this was a new ho.

She sat up in the bed and continued to rub in between her legs, sucking on her bottom lip. "Simone bought me a week

33

ago, and I've only been working for her for two days. You're my third trick, but the first one that actually fucked me. The first two just held me and did some other kinky things that weren't really sexual. Well, not for me, at least. My mother owed her over ten thousand dollars for a heroin debt, and she paid her off with me. So, I guess this is my home now. It sucks, but at least here I get to have three meals and a bed to sleep in." She stood up and tried to slip into her ripped panties, but it was no use. They were through. "Why do you want to know so much about me?" she asked, giving me a look of amusement.

There was a knock on the door and Simone stuck her head in. "Time's up, lover boy. She needs to get showered and be ready for her next appointment in an hour, and me and you need to handle a little unfinished business." She smiled, opening the door a little wider.

I looked down the hall and saw a redbone who couldn't have been any older than fifteen leading a portly old man into a room by the hand. Before they made it all the way inside, he smacked her on the ass, causing her to yelp out loud.

I shook my head. "That ain't happening. I'm taking her wit' me." I turned to look at Tracy. "Grab all of yo' shit and let's go, now!"

She looked at Simone like a deer caught in headlights. "What?"

Simone stepped forward with a frown on her face. "Nall, Shotgun, you not finna do me like this. I just got this li'l girl, and I can already tell she gon' be one of my best money-makers. She loves sex, she's fine, and she's built. Mix all of that with the fact she looks fourteen in the face and you gotta be crazy if you think I'ma let this happen."

I turned my head sideways and mugged the shit out of her before setting my bag on the floor, going inside of it, and pulling out my police-issued Glock .40. Then I stood up and grabbed her by the blouse while Tracy screamed behind me. I placed the .40 to Simone's forehead. "Bitch, did you forget

I'm the muthafuckin' police? Or did you forget I'm Shotgun?" I asked, twisting the barrel into her skin harshly.

She started to shake, taking her hand and pushing out against me to create space. "Shotgun, what the fuck are you doing? I been knowing you for twenty years. You gon' do me like this? Over her?"

I could hear her voice cracking up, and I didn't give no fucks. I wanted Tracy. She was the closest thing I'd seen to Leesee in a long time, it felt. I needed her to act as my knock-off baby girl until I could find the real her.

"Bitch, I ain't doing shit to you. I want her, and that's what I'm finna get. I'll give you the ten gees her mother owed you, plus the one from me handling my bitness wit' her today. On top of that, its girls being snatched up by the state every single day. I'll do what I gotta do to make sure the next three that look like somethin' are snatched up and placed here permanently. Now, that's the best I can do. Take that shit or leave it, but no matter what, you lost this one. She belongs to me." I yanked on her hair. "Do you hear me?"

"Uh! Yeah, fuck. I hear you, Shotgun. It all sounds good. Just pay me my money and get her out of here. The next three that come through the system, they belong to me. That's our deal. Cool?" She extended her hand so I could shake it.

Out of the corner of my eye I saw her big, beefy, black-ass bodyguard creeping down the hall with a baseball bat. I flung her to the floor and aimed at him. As soon as he saw me, he threw his arms in the air.

"Bring yo' big, bitch ass down here, nigga. Hurry up, before I pop yo' stupid ass. Run!"

He got to running down the hall toward us with his stomach bouncing up and down along with his man-titties. When he got to the room, I grabbed him and smacked him so hard he flew into the door, holding his face.

"Punk-ass nigga. Fuck you think you gon' do wit' a baseball bat, huh?" I ran forward and kneed him in the chest, making him fall to his ass, then I put the pistol to his temple.

Simone stood up with her hands in front of her. "Shotgun, please, just take this girl and leave. You can give me the money at another time. It's not important right now. We don't want no trouble. Matter fact, Tracy is on the house if you leave right now. You won't owe me one red cent. How does that sound?" She looked from me to her bodyguard. His head was bent awkwardly, sweat pouring down his face, and dripping off of his chin.

I looked past her to Tracy. "Let's go, baby girl. You can leave all that shit, 'cause you already got a whole wardrobe at home."

Love Me Even When It Hurts 2

Chapter 4

Leesee

Two months had passed since we'd heard anything from either Shotgun or Sharome's brother, Kazi. I was starting to think we were in the clear, but I knew better, and I was sure prayin' every single night that God was watching over us and protecting us from those beasts of men.

Rah'nell called in a few favors and got us linked up with one of his old running partners by the name of Ramsey. He was a major hustler out in Harlem and well respected in the game. Rah'nell said back in the day he and Shotgun were always at war with each other's crews, and even to this day they hated each other, so we'd never have to worry about him screwing us over. I didn't get many bad vibes from the man, and as far as I could tell neither did Sharome. In fact, it didn't take long before Ramsey helped him become deeply embedded within the dope game out in Harlem. They seemed to get along real well, and more often than not whenever Sharome was in the streets, he was always with Ramsey.

We wound up renting out a two-story apartment: me, Sharome, and we allowed my cousin Tia to move in with us, though we gave her the space upstairs. According to her there were still a bunch of dudes looking for her in connection to Pappy's murder. They felt she'd been the one to set him up because something like that happened with her and an old boyfriend she'd supposedly gotten set up to be robbed and murdered. I didn't know how true that rumor was, but it did have me a bit on edge.

I had a timetable in my head when I was going to ask her to move out, but first I wanted her to gather herself and get her head back. We had all been through a lot within the past few months.

Jelissa

I was taking classes online to become a childcare professional. I wanted to work with kids because I'd always had a passion for that field. I saw myself owning a few daycares where I'd make sure my children were well taken care of at all times. While I was taking classes online, I was also writing my second book. A story about my life, though I was writing it with a fictitious twist.

I loved writing. On most days when I was going through bout after bout of mental pains, writing was the only escape for me. It allowed me to go to a place I'd created. I was missing my mother, sister, and grandparents more and more lately, and I was more than sure all four of them were no longer living. There had been no activity on any of their social media accounts, and ten times both me and Sharome had been out to my grandparents' home only to receive no answer from them, though of their cars were in the garage. Every family member I'd reached out to had not heard from them, either, and the last I heard they were going to have the local authorities go over and kick in the door. My cousin Shante had told me this yesterday, and I had yet to hear back about the results. But, to be quite honest, I was so worried about what the truth would be that I almost didn't want to know what she found out.

Thursday morning, Sharome woke me up by kissing along my toes and all the way up my ankles until he was sucking on my right calf muscle. "Wake up, baby. Wake up and let me see that pretty face before I hit these streets," he said, continuing on his course up my body.

I felt him move my thighs apart, and then his face was under my gown and in my crease with his tongue licking up and down my center. "Mm, baby, what are you doing?" I moaned, arching my back, my eyes shooting wide open, seeing the top of his waves.

He slurped up my juices. "I been missing you, baby. I been out all night. Now I wanna taste my woman. Huh, this for you," he said, handing me a red rose and a jewelry box before diving back between my legs and really going to town on me. I felt him open my kitty lips and trap my clitoris inside of his thick lips, sucking on her for dear life.

I placed the bottoms of my feet on the bed and humped into his mouth with my eyes rolling into the back of my head. "Uh, uh, uh. Ooh. Ah, uh! Baby, it feels so good." I placed my thighs on his shoulders and forced his face deeper into my box, grinding into it, feeling the waves of my orgasm speeding toward me.

He licked wildly, and sucked, slurped up my juices and attacked my clitty again and again, driving me out of my mind. I could barely take it as I humped into him with my feet in the air. Then the tremors started. Oh my god, this man knew how to eat me like no other. I didn't understand how he'd learned me so quick.

"Ah! Baby, I'm cumming already. Ooh, shit, Sharome, I'm cumming all over you baby!" I screamed and started to hump his face a hunnit miles an hour while his fingers dug into my thighs and his face went deeper into my middle, sucking and eating for all he was worth.

Afterward, he sat on the bed and lifted my feet into his lap. "G'on 'head, baby, check out yo' gift. I hope you like it."

He lifted my right foot to his lips and kissed the toes before setting it back down, rubbing them both. He seemed to love my li'l feet, and that made me feel so good. Just the fact this man paid so much attention to every little detail of me made me feel so special and wanted. And he wasn't doing it because I resembled someone else. No, he was doing it because he was enamored with me and only me.

I picked up the red rose and sniffed it, smiling and looking at him with appreciation. "Thank you for the rose, baby. I really appreciate you. You make me feel so good, honest." I leaned forward and kissed his lips, tasting my essence upon them.

"It's good, baby. Everything I do out there is for you. I just wanna heal you in every way I can, because you mean the world to me. I love you with all my heart, Leesee, fo' real. Now open it up. I wanna see if you like it."

I nodded, took a deep breath, and exhaled, opening Jared's box, to reveal a gold chain and heart that had pink diamonds iced all around it. I took it all the way out of the box and held it in my hand, watching it twinkle in the light. It was so beautiful I wanted to cry. I didn't think I deserved anything as beautiful as that. I felt my throat get tight. "Sharome, I can't keep this. It must've cost you a fortune. You're already paying all of the bills, and you just bought me a Lexus. Baby, you're doing way too much. I feel like I'm using you, and that's not cool." I placed the jewelry back into the box and closed it, handing it over to him.

He lightly pushed my hand, then pulled it so I was kissing his lips. He sucked on my bottom one playfully for a short time before letting it go, standing up, and pulling out a big knot of hundreds. "Man, we good, baby. You see all this cash? Yo' man is out here in Harlem eating like crazy. That nigga Ramsey is the truth. I'm all up and down Lenox eating wit' them Blood niggaz, and they been so one hunnit." He took the .9 millimeter out of the small of his back and sat it on the dresser, leaned down, and pulled out another knot of hundreds and fifties, tossing it on the bed between my thighs. "That's for you, right there. It should be about eleven bands. I want you to put it up in case of an emergency. This right here is for your pocket. He peeled off a gee and gave it to me, then put the rest back into his pocket. "I gotta take you to get yo' hair and nails done, too. It's been about two weeks, ain't it?" he asked, taking his white t-shirt off and tossing it on the bed.

I stood up and stretched my arms over my head, then looked at my fingernails. They still looked brand new. It had only been ten days since I'd got them done. "Nall, baby, it's only been ten days. They still good," I said, rubbing my baby hairs along my forehead.

Love Me Even When It Hurts 2

He unsnapped his bulletproof vest and dropped it on the floor. "Nall, that ain't cool. That fool Ramsey be getting his wife's nails done every week. I gotta step my game up. I know he don't love her half as much as I love you. That nigga still getting pussy on the side. I'm loyal to my baby, so I gotta step it up." He turned around to face me. His body was ripped up, stomach muscles popping like all he did all day was sit-ups. He reached and wrapped his arms around my upper back and pulled me into him, lowering his head so he could press his forehead up against mine. I looked into his gray eyes and felt butterflies in my stomach. This man had that effect on me. For the first time in my life I was actually able to understand what love really meant. I took a deep breath and found myself intoxicated by the scent of him. He smelled of Polo cologne and just a tad bit of manly sweat. The pheromones coming off of him were doing somethin' to my middle.

He kissed my lips softly. "You know I love you, right?"

I nodded my head and continued to look into his sexy eyes. "Yeah, baby, I do. Why you ask me that?" I was praying he wasn't saying that in the one breath, and then in the next about to drop some form of a bomb shell on me. I don't know why, but every single day I found myself worried one day he would snap out of the zone I had him in, and then he'd no longer see me the way he saw me. I didn't feel like any man could love me as much as Sharome did. I still didn't understand why he loved me so freaking much. I felt like there was nothin' really special about me, that a man like him could have any female he really wanted at any time, and I was at the bottom of the barrel. I didn't know what he saw in me, but every single day I felt a little more confident within myself, but more and more afraid he'd leave once he found somethin' or someone better than me. I had no worth, and not really much to offer him as a woman, and that scared me. He was a go-getter. Everything he wanted or needed he went out and got on his own while I stayed home.

Jelissa

He held me a more firmly and kissed my lips again. "Yo',
I been thinking like I been neglecting you, ma, and I gotta
change that. I love you with all of my heart, and I gotta make
sure you know that at all times. So, what I want you to do is
think about anywhere you wanna go, or anything you wanna
do, and I'll make it happen. I'ma go out here and hustle all
week so the money won't be a problem. I gotta spoil my baby.
You're all I got and all I need. You're my everything, word is
bond."

I felt myself getting weak in the knees. It seemed like he
was always saying and doing the things that spoke directly to
my heart. He made me so emotional, so thrown off. Around
him I could barely think straight. He loved me so much, and
that was foreign to me. I didn't feel like I deserved his type of
love. I exhaled loudly and looked into his eyes, not knowing
what to say or do. I was stuck.

He picked me up out of nowhere, causing me to yelp out
loud before wrapping my legs around him. I held onto his big,
well-defined arms and felt his abs all up against my kitty. This
close he smelled even better. I felt my middle purring for him
again, and I just couldn't control my urges.

He held me for a short time, just twisting me from side to
side while he hugged me, his eyes were closed, and he just
kept on inhaling and exhaling. "I never wanna fail you, baby.
You deserve the absolute best of the best, and it's my job to
make sure you have it. You're my sole purpose in this world.
I need you more and more every single day." He tightened his
hug while I lay my head on his shoulder.

I felt my eyes getting watery and I was trying everything I
could to not allow a tear to fall. "Sharome, do you think you
will always love me? I'm talking like ten years from now?" I
asked, feeling real emotional.

He exhaled loudly. "There is no life without you, Leesee.
You give me a reason to wake up in the morning. There was
nobody that loved me be 'fore you. Nobody, baby. Then you
came along, and you're showing me what this love thing is all

about, and I need it so bad in my life. You are it. I'll be loving you for as long as there is breath in my body. I promise, ma." He kissed my neck and rubbed his cheek up against my own before laying his face in the groove of my shoulder and neck. "I never wanna fail you, baby. I'll do anything for you, or about you. You're my everything. I mean that with all I am as a man. I grind for you first, and then myself. Word is bond."

He continued to hold me up while I felt like a big-ass, loved baby. All of this man was crazy about me, and I didn't know how to accept it. I was so used to being used or made out to be somebody I wasn't. I didn't understand his obsession, but I was so thankful for it as a woman. I needed it just as bad as he needed me.

He put me down and brushed my curls out of my face, smiling. Both dimples appearing on his cheeks. "I want you to go get your fingers and toes done and see if you can have a spa day today. I'll handle that off of my credit card. I just need for my baby to relax and let loose all afternoon, cuz tonight I'ma take you out to dinner and just chill. I wanna hear what's on your mind, and we still gotta figure out what college you going to. Just 'cause I'm in these streets don't mean our dreams have to die. Somebody gotta pull us outta the slums."

I smiled and wrapped my arms around the top of his neck. "Baby, you're something else, you know that? You always putting me first. I don't know what I did to deserve you, but all I can say is Jehovah is real." I sucked his lips into my mouth and smiled.

He laughed. "That's my job. I gotta take care of my baby."

"Damn, what about me?" Tia said, stepping into the room and crossin' her arms in front of her chest. She had on some real tight denim shorts that had her chocolate thighs on full display. Her pink wife beater was cut so it showcased her stomach muscles, and she was barefoot. *Way too comfortable to be downstairs* was my first thought. I wondered if Sharome ever felt some type of way about her. I think it would have been hard not too. I had to admit she was gorgeous.

Sharome released me and laughed. "Aw, you already know I got you, too, Tia. I can't leave you out in the cold like that. My baby would kill me, huh, ma?" he asked, looking down at me.

I almost blurted out hell nall, I wouldn't, but I kept it classy and simply smiled. "Tia, what, you can't knock no more?" I asked, flaring my nostrils. I peeped more than once the way she looked Sharome up and down. I knew she had to be drinking in his rock-hard body, and that made me super jealous. I wanted to punch her ass in the nose. I needed to be held my man some more, and now that she was in the room it made me feel tense and on guard.

She sucked her teeth and waved me off. "Gurl, stop playin'. Since when we knocking on doors and shit? Y'all ain't got nothin' I ain't seen before. Plus, this door was already open damn near all the way." She rolled her eyes and shook her head.

I almost took offense to that, but once again I had to keep my composure.

Sharome kissed my neck, then stepped to the side, and I watched her walk into his arms and hug him. Before I could even stop myself, I stepped forward and broke that shit up, pulling their shoulders apart. Especially since she closed her eyes once he embraced her. Oh, hell nall. "Un-uh, ain't none of that shit. Sharome, you betta go put a shirt on before you call yourself huggin' on my cousin. Ain't nobody supposed to be feeling that heat but me." I looked at him with my forehead scrunched. I was getting pissed.

He laughed and must've thought I was playing. "Aw, shit. Damn, Tia, I guess you see what it is. The wifey ain't going."

Tia frowned and placed her hand on her hip. "Damn, why you trippin' all the sudden, Leesee? I been hugging him every day, now all the sudden it's a problem?" She looked to me, and then started to trail her eyes up and down his body again. I caught it plain as day this time, and I wasn't exaggerating.

Then she had the nerve to bite on her bottom lip while she ogled him as if she didn't know what to do with herself.

I picked up Sharome's shirt and tossed it to him. "Huh, put that on. And you, wait in the living room for us. We'll be out there in a minute." I walked to the door and opened it wider for her to walk out of.

As she stepped past me, she looked me up and down. "You trippin', Leesee. I don't know what's going on wit' you all of the sudden, but trust me, it ain't that kind of party when it comes to Sharome. He's like my brother." She looked over my shoulder toward him. "Yo, when you ready, I need you to drop me off in the hood at Nell's spot. She wants me to do her hair, and she's willin' to pay me $200. I need those ends, but I'm supposed to meet her within the next hour, if that's cool?"

I turned to look at him, and he looked at the floor. "Yo, it's good wit' me, but it's up to my baby. Somethin' ain't right wit' her, so let me see what's good, then I'll come let you know. Just hold on a minute." He grabbed me by my gown and pulled me to him as Tia walked out of the door and closed it behind her, shaking her head in obvious anger.

I knocked his hands away and turned my back on him. "You ever look at her in that way before?" I asked, feeling vulnerable as hell. I didn't know what was going on. I think I was jealous of my cousin's body or something.

He exhaled and rolled his head around on his neck. "Leesee why we gotta go there?" He ran his hand over the top of his deep waves, then opened the dresser drawer, taking out a pair of Tom Ford boxers.

I came and stood beside him. "Nall, fo' real, Sharome. I want you to be honest with me. Have you ever looked at her in that way?"

He took his thumb and forefinger and pinched the top of his nose with his eyes closed. "In what way is that, Leesee? And please keep in mind I don't wanna do this. I feel like we in a good space, and you finna ruin it."

I brushed that crap off. I wasn't trying to hear that. As a woman, I just needed to know. "Anyway, have you ever desired her before? Have you ever looked at her in a lustful manner? Be honest."

He shook his head. "Man, I ain't never lied to you before, and I never will, but you can't be asking me questions you really don't want the answers to."

I stepped into his face. "Sharome, the truth." I took a deep breath and exhaled loudly.

Chapter 5

Rome

"Baby, yo' cousin decent looking, and she got a li'l body on her, so yeah, I done looked at her in that way before. But I'd never and haven't ever thought about crossin' them lines with her. I love you way too much, and I'm more of a man than that. Believe me when I tell you that."

Leesee looked up at me and curled her upper lip. She stood staring for a long time without saying a word. "You know what? I need to clear my head. You can drop her off wherever you need too, and then you and I can link up later sometime if you feel like it. Right now, my mind is spinning." She blew air from between her teeth and walked off, shaking her head.

I grabbed her arm and turned her around. "What's wrong wit' you? What, you would have preferred if I lied or somethin'?"

She looked at me very calmly, and then looked down at where I was holding her. "Sharome, let my arm go. I need to gather my thoughts, and I'll get at you a li'l later."

I released her arm and turned my back on her, snatching me a Tom Ford fit out of the closet and a pair of Jordans. I felt like being in the hood and getting money after I grabbed a quick shower. I didn't know what was going on with her, but I had to respect her enough to give her space.

When I got outside, Tia was waiting for me, sitting on the hood of my Cadillac STS with her li'l shorts on. As soon as I came out of the house she started smiling. I unlocked the doors from my key controls, walked around, and hopped into the driver's seat after she opened the door for me. I started the ignition and pulled away from the curb, still a little angry from my exchange with Leesee.

She shook her head. "Hm, mm, mm. That girl got a good ass, man, and she gon' wind up trickin' you off because she don't know how to handle her emotions." She fixed her seatbelt around her and looked over to me. "You okay? I ain't never seen you look this angry before."

Even though I was heated, I faked the funk. "I'm good. I just don't understand women sometimes. I'm tryna do everything I can for her, and it seem like no matter what I do, I always manage to fuck up and piss her off. I love that girl, man. She all I got in this world." I jumped on the highway and increased my speed, pulling out the ashtray and grabbing the blunt out of it and lighting it.

"Nah, kid, that's where you wrong at. She ain't the only one you got in this world. You got me, too, and I love you whether you believe it or not. It's time you acknowledge that, though." She reached over, squeezed my thigh, and smiled.

I shook my head. "Well, you need to tell me what I should do to make her happy, because obviously I'm dropping the ball on a regular basis. It's getting to the point I don't know what to do. I hate feeling defeated, especially when it comes to her. I love your cousin, Tia, fo' real."

Tia nodded her head. "I know you do, and that's why I'm here for y'all. I'll help you figure things out. Don't worry, we got this. I promise, okay?" She leaned over and kissed my cheek, then wiped it away with her thumb.

I nodded. "Yeah, a'ight, long as you got my back. Don't let me fumble. Make sure I stay on my game when it comes to her, and I got you. Anything you need, just let me know," I said, pullin' up in front of Nell's crib. I went into my pocket and pulled out the gee I'd brought out of the house wit' me. "Huh, here you go, three hunnit bucks. Once you make that two hunnit in there, that'll give you five hunnit even. A woman should never have less than five hunnit dollars in pocket change. That's just how I feel. Anytime you get low, you let me know and I got you, ma, word is bond." I handed her the money.

She took it and lowered her head, then leaned across the seat and hugged my neck. "I swear to God I'd do anything to have a man like you. These dudes out here are trifling. They don't care about us women out here. You are rare, and like I said, I love you to death. I mean that shit." She kissed my cheek again, and then opened the passenger's door and got out. I couldn't miss the fact her denim shorts were all in her ass, exposing both dark brown cheeks. I couldn't do nothin' but shake my head as I drove away.

Fifteen minutes later, and after a brief stop at the Gyro Shack, I pulled up in front of the apartment complex Ramsey had just bought for us to move heroin and meth out of. There were about ten Blood niggaz standing in front of it wit' red rags around their necks and pistols under their shirts. I could tell because I could see the handles of the guns sticking out.

I parked my whip and jumped out just as Ramsey was coming out of the building. He was about five feet, nine inches tall and real muscular, with a gut though, and long cornrows that fell past his chest. He was light-skinned with brown eyes. As soon as he saw me, he smiled and walked over with a big blunt in his hand. Two Blood niggaz walked close behind him on security.

He switched the blunt from his right hand over to his left so we could embrace with half-hugs. "Sharome, what it do, kid?"

I hugged him and stood back. "It's good. I'm ready to feed off the slums, Boss. My lady wilding out. Word is bond, I need an escape," I said as he wrapped his arm around my shoulder and led me into the building. As we crossed the threshold of the complex, there were three dudes in the hallway with pistols out and mugs on their faces. They had red rags around their necks and gave me a "what up" nod when our eyes met. "What up, Slime?" I said, and they threw up the Peru Blood sign. I wasn't officially plugged into their mob and I didn't know if I ever was going to plug into them. I was about money. I didn't care about no color but green. I thought all that gang-

49

Jelissa

banging shit was stupid, but I was eating wit' them niggaz, which meant if some shit kicked off, I was gon' bust my gun until it was empty. I pledged my loyalty to Ramsey, and he was a Blood, so I guess in a sense his enemies were mine, point-blank.

We went up two flights of stairs and wound up in the apartment where we moved that Fentanyl out of. Ramey's bodyguards closed the door behind us. I stepped into the apartment and damn near fainted because it was so funky. I mean it smelled like ass, fish, and musk. That shit had me gagging, but all he did was laugh.

All around the room were dope addicts about thirty deep. They were lying on the floor, sitting up against the wall doing their dope. Some were helping others find a vein in their arms or legs, and I even saw one female getting her dope injected into her kat. That blew my mind. I looked around me and basically saw what I thought hell would look like. The smell was so pungent I was about to pass out.

I followed Ramsey into the back of the apartment, where he knocked on a door. The person on the other side asked who it was. "It's Ramsey the God, nigga. Open this muthafuckin' door so I can check my bread." He took a step back with a mug on his face.

The door opened, and there was a wave of funk that hit me so hard I fell backward and threw up in my mouth a li'l bit. I pulled my shirt over my nose and looked forward before following him into the room. There were dope addicts fucking the shit out of each other all around this room. They were naked, huffing and puffing, and smelling like a sewer system. I looked down and saw the condition of some of the underwear of the addicts, and I just felt grossed out completely.

Ramsey lay his hand on my shoulder. "This what that good dope do to a hype, Sharome. This is one of our oasis rooms. Dope fiends give us they whole check to be in this muthafucka for three hours a day. In here you can fuck, shoot dope, or get fucked while you shot up wit' dope. It's about twenty people

in here, and ain't no one gave us no less than seven hunnit."
He wrapped his arm around my neck as the dude in charge of
the operation in that room handed him a big bundle of cash
with a rubber band around it. He took it and put it in his inside
jacket pocket before leading me out of there. I was happy, too,
because I was seconds away from throwing up on the couple
of dudes who were tag-teaming one skinny female addict who
looked sick.

I followed him as he made his rounds all around the
building, collecting his paper. About an hour after I arrived,
we wound up in his Bentley truck with Nas rapping out of the
speakers and two bodyguards standing outside of the truck on
point.

He turned to me and handed me a Garcia y Vega green-
leafed cigar stuffed with Miami Dro. I took the blunt and
pulled off it two quick times, inhaling deeply.

Ramsey took his Sprite and poured two bottles of sizzurp
into it before shaking it up. Then he crushed two oxycodone
pills on a CD case and snorted the powder from it, saving half
for me.

I politely pushed his hand away. "Nall, I'm good, Boss.
Last time I tried that shit I couldn't keep my eyes open. This
bud is enough for me, word is bond, and it's taking a toll."

Ramsey leaned his head down and tooted up the lines he'd
left over for me. Pinching his nose, he unscrewed the top to
the Sprite and turned it up, swallowing like it wasn't nothin'.
"Yo, that's why I fuck wit' you, Sharome. Son, every nigga
that been in the game as long as I have need a li'l young
souljah wit' smarts to be his eyes." He wiped his mouth and
screwed the top back on the bottle. "I wanna see you eating,
my nigga, an I'm finna help you turn up. Let's roll for a
minute." He let his window down and stuck his head out.
"Say, kid, I need one car in front of me and another in back.
I'm finna lace my li'l nigga and get him right, so I need
privacy in here. I roll out in two minutes. Let's go."

Jelissa

He reached under his seat and pulled up a Mach .90, cocked it, and handed it to me. "You see anything that look fishy, you murk that shit. We got beef with a few decks, and these niggaz in Harlem is snakes. Muthafuckas quick to blindside you, so to be aware is to stay alive. Nah mean?"

I slid my hands into black leather gloves and nodded my head. I was ready to wet anybody Ramsey told me to. I had his back and I would follow his command wit' no hesitation.

He placed another Mach on his lap after cocking it. "Yo, reason I wanna rollout wit' you is 'cuz got some bitness for you I only want you to handle since you got a clear head and don't fuck with these drugs, nah mean?" He grabbed a Kleenex from a small box that sat in the middle of us and wiped his nose because it was constantly dripping. On top of that, his voice had gotten raspy and slow.

"Yo, word is bond, I'm down to do whatever you need me to do, big homie. I'm trying to eat and feed my peoples by any means."

He nodded his head as the sun beamed through the windshield. I had to flip down the visor and lower my eyes. Ramsey reached across me, popped open his glove box, and pulled out a pair of Cartier shades, putting them on. I had to admit the old head had plenty of swag.

He made a right and stormed down a side street. "Starting Friday I'ma be fucking with one of the Haitian bosses down in Miami. They been plugging us real hard on the heroin, and I'ma return that favor by sending a few loads of meth their way. I got these Arian white boys that know how to whip a bathtub of that shit in four days. Off of that we ain't seeing no less than five hunnit thousand, and that's after I take care of the Haitians."

He smiled and turned the music down, beeping the horn at a thick-ass redbone who was on her way to getting into a pink drop-top Mercedes Benz. She had on a tight yellow Fendi dress that had her ass looking right. I felt guilty for even peeping all that, but I did.

52

She looked over her shoulder at Ramsey's passing Bentley and smiled before opening her car door and getting inside of it.

Ramsey shook his head. "It's so many hoez out here, li'l bruh, that it's hard to stay faithful. Lord knows I been trying." He laughed, adjusted his sun visor, and sipped from his pink Sprite. "Anyway, like I was saying, them white boys'll whip that work every four days and hit us wit' a nice batch we can send down to Miami. I guess Sycleff, the Haitian boss out that way, trying to expand his operations. That meth shit is on the rise down there, and my white boys make the best glass on the east coast for a li'l of this and that. They gon' keep me straight, and in turn I'ma keep Sycleff straight, and vice versa. It's a lot of money to be made, and I'm trying to have my hand in every circle that gon' get and keep me and my niggaz rich, you feel me?"

I was hearing everything he was saying, but I wanted to know where I fit in with all of this. "So, what's good wit' me?" I asked, situating the Mach on my lap and looking out my window for predators. I peeped our rearview mirror and saw a van of Bloodz were following close behind his Bentley, and there was another van-full right in front of us.

He grunted. "Kid, I'm about to line yo' pockets wit' plenty green. You finna eat until you burp, son, word is bond. You see, you gon' be my traveler. I'ma have you make all of the drop-offs and meet wit' each of the bosses, or the ones the bosses have in charge of their distributions. You'll pick up the meth and bring that over straight to Harlem. Once you get to me, I'll take the amount that's staying in Harlem and send you wit' the rest that goes to Sycleff down in Miami. Now, when you get to him, he gon' swap out the meth with his high-grade heroin. One hand will wash the other. You'll bring the heroin back to Harlem, and so forth and so on. This'll happen every four days, or every time my white boys finish a batch of ice. I'ma pay you ten bands to take the work to Miami, and another ten to bring back whatever he send up." He sucked his teeth loudly and smiled. "How does that sound to you?"

I got to imagining having twenty stacks every four days, and I was already spending the paper in my head. I would surely be able to make some things happen for Leesee and myself. I knew I wanted her to enroll in a real university so she could get a good education. She wanted to do that and was thinking of filing for financial aid, but I advised against it once I heard how that whole process was designed to put people into financial slavery. I didn't want her caught up like that, and I felt I was man enough to send her to school on my own so she could become whatever she wanted to. She was my woman, and I felt like it was my job to make sure she was straight all around the board. I would do whatever it took.

The moves that Ramsey wanted me to make sounded good. That was nice money, and in order for me to have seen any type of numbers like that I would've had to sit in a trap house for months at a time and save my paper. That was unrealistic.

I turned to him and nodded my head. "What that security detail gon' be like, though?" I had to remember that just like the game had hustlers, they also had jackers – niggaz that fed their family by laying kats down like me who were in the drug industry.

Ramsey curled his upper lip as he pulled into a car lot that showcased newly-released whips. "Yo, you tell me what you need to make it happen, and I got you. My only thing is I don't want none of the niggaz in my circle knowin' what I'm doing, so you might have to bring in a few niggaz you trust to tail you from a distance. All I can say is I'm more than sure you ain't gon' have no problems for a while, long as you stick to the script. Oh, and you gon' need a li'l bitch to push the whip for you. One that got her license and insurance. You know, just to throw the Jakes off of you. Nah mean? So, what's good? You fuckin' wit' me or not?" he asked, pulling into a vacant parking spot.

Love Me Even When It Hurts 2

Two hours later I was sitting behind the steering wheel of a black-on-black 2020 Benz truck.

"Yo, kid, this is what I call a signing bonus. This you right here, and you don't owe me nothin'. This just from fucking with the God, nah mean? I'ma get everything together on my end, and you do the same. Be ready to roll out in three days. Time is money."

Jelissa

Chapter 6

Leesee

It had been two days since I'd really been myself or had been lovey-dovey toward Sharome, and I think it was getting the better of him because all he did was walk around the house in silence with his head down. Tia didn't say much, either, whenever we did cross paths, and I guessed she was salty at me or somethin', but I really didn't care. I felt like she'd overstepped her bounds two days ago, and that was that. If she was feeling some type of way about the things I'd said, I felt she should have brought them to my attention like a woman. So, I really wasn't worried about her. I was worried about my man and where we stood with one another.

Sharome came into the house at around nine o'clock Thursday night with a book bag on his shoulder. After he closed the door behind him, he kicked off his Timbs and walked into the living room, where he unzipped the bag after sitting down on the couch. Then I watched him place stack after stack of money on top of the glass table.

"Look, this li'l paper should help you with yo' tuition fees. I don't know what college you trying to get into right now, but this paper should definitely help. It's twenty gees, and it's all yours."

After he said this, he zipped the book bag and stood up, not even looking me in the eye and heading toward the back of the house where our bedroom was located. I watched him pause as he got to the door, then he looked over his shoulder at me with a curious look on his face.

I covered the space in between us quickly. As soon as I was in his face, I looked into his eyes and sucked on my bottom lip, allowing the silk robe to fall off my shoulders and body, leaving me standing there in my red-and-black micro Victoria's Secret nightgown.

He looked down on me. "Baby, what's all of this? I hope it's for me and you weren't expectin' company?" He flared his nostrils, then turned to face the room I'd decked out in red rose petals and scented pink candles.

Coming out of the speakers were the sounds of SZA, and I was needing my man in the worst way. I was trying to not allow his last comment to throw me out of my mood, because it almost did. He should have known I would have never thought to bring anybody into our bedroom. I loved him way too much for that. I sighed and stood on my tippy-toes, turning him around to face me. "Baby, I love you, and I'm sorry. I didn't mean to act the way I did toward you. I know you love me to death and you only see me. I appreciate that so fucking much, you have no idea. Come here."

I took his hand and pulled him further into the room. He followed close behind with a serious look on his face. "Yo, you my baby. I ain't sweating that. I just gotta prove myself to you a li'l more so you'll know you really are all I see. I'd do anything for you. I need you to know that."

I walked up to him and kissed his lips, at the same time forcing him to walk backward until he fell on his butt on top of our bed that was covered in rose petals, then I knelt down in front of him.

"It's time baby. I know you wanted to wait until your official birthday, but fuck that. I can't take it anymore. I need you inside of me. I need you to possess me in the way a man should." I started to unbuckle his Gucci belt, and then got to working his shorts off of him. Next came his boxers. His big dick sprang out and nearly slapped me on the cheek. I grabbed it in my little fist and started to pump it up and down, looking him in the gray eyes and running my tongue across my lips. "You goin' in me tonight, and I ain't tryna hear nothin'. Now that you out there in them streets, it's finna be plenty bitchez that's gon' wanna throw you the kat, and I can't have you

58

falling to temptation. I gotta handle my bitness as a woman. I know what type of man you are, and I can't lose you." I opened my mouth and sucked him into it, taking his pipe halfway down, then bringing my lips back to his tip, twirling my tongue around it like a pro. For some reason every time I tasted him it made me weak and highly sexual. I speared my head into his lap again and again while he groaned and squeezed his eyelids together. I took that as a sign I was doing my thing.

"Mm, damn, ma. Yo. Shit. That feel so good," he groaned, raising his ass from the bed so he could go deeper into my mouth. I rolled with the punches. Every time he raised his hips, I allowed his pipe to go all the way down my throat, then I'd bring his dick back out of it. I sucked on the head for a long time, then began stroking him again. "A'right, Sharome. I want you to fuck me now. I need you to put it down, baby, okay? Don't play wit' me." I crawled on the bed and lay on my back, pulling my gown up so he could see my naked pussy dripping its juices in anticipation for him. I needed his body bad. My walls were actually throbbing and jumping for him.

He took his shirt off to reveal his rock-hard body, then knelt before me, placing my thighs on each side of him before pickin' up the right leg and holding it in his forearm. I reached in between us, took his fat helmet, and slowly slid it through my sex lips. As each inch traveled through my hole, my body began to shake more and more. When I felt there was about four inches left, I arched my back. "Baby, slam the rest of that in there hard. Please. I need to feel you. I love you so much."

He cocked back and slammed it forward with authority, just the way I needed him to. I hollered and closed my eyes, sucking on my bottom lip. "Yes, baby, just like that. Now fuck me as hard as you can. Go, baby!" I arched my back and reached out for his waist.

Sharome started to move in and out of me at a steady pace, sexing me as a tender lover, and I prayed he would turn into a savage. It felt good, don't get me wrong, but I needed him to really put it down like a beast.

He leaned forward and sucked on my neck. "This shit so good, baby. Uh. Uh. Uh. Uh. Damn, this pussy so good. I love you. Mm, shit!"

He sped up the pace, and I could feel his pipe reaching the bottom of my womb. I curled my toes and rubbed all over his abs. That always drove me nuts. "Mm, fuck me, baby! Fuck me harder, please! I need you to kill this pussy. Hit it like you need me!" I screamed, opening my legs wide to allow him the room to do whatever he needed to. "Harder, Sharome!"

He started to put his back into it, going deeper and deeper. "Uh. Uh. Uh. Mm. Leesee. I'm finna cum. I'm finna cum, baby. This shit so good. It's so good. Fuck!" he hollered, fucking into me at full speed, and then I felt his body tense up before the hot squirts of his semen shot into me over and over.

He lay on top of me with his penis still throbbing deep within my womb. It didn't feel like it lost any of its length, and I knew I had to take advantage of that because I needed to cum so bad. I'd not gotten there yet. I sat up. "Baby, put your hand around my neck and choke me a li'l bit so I can get there." I said, feeling my box ooze my juices out of it. I needed some relief. I was about to scream if I didn't get some.

Sharome frowned. "What?"

I felt myself blush. I was seconds away from telling him it was alright, but then my kat jumped again. "You heard me, baby. I just like to be choked a li'l bit. It helps me get off. You ain't gotta kill me or nothin'." I laughed nervously. "I just wanna feel your need for me. A need that would drive you to do whatever it takes to get in between my legs."

He looked me over for a long time, and then sat on the side of the bed. "I don't know about that, Leesee. I ain't trying to hurt you or no shit like that. I thought we was just fucking like normal people," he said, looking me in the eyes.

I lowered my head and thought, d*amn, so now I ain't normal?* My feelings were hurt. I wished I'd never brought it

up. I was feeling like a fool. I nodded my head. "It's good, baby. Don't worry about it. I should have never said nothin'."
I scooted until I was sitting on the other side of the bed with my head lowered. I didn't know what he was thinking of me, but I felt like crap.

He stood up and walked around to my side, looking down at me. "Hey, I didn't mean anything by that. You just threw me off a li'l bit. I didn't know that some females needed to be choked in order to get off. That's my bad. I'll do it, come on." He placed his hands on each of my shoulders.

I knocked them away. "Nall, I said it's good." I stood up with my face blushing. "I just wanted to try somethin wit' you. I don't need to be choked in order to get off, either, it just would have heightened my arousal." I walked into the bathroom and closed the door, sliding down it until I was sitting on my butt.

Sharome knocked on it about two minutes later, scaring the hell out of me. "Leesee, I'm sorry, baby. You know I'm new to this whole fucking thing. It's a lot of stuff I don't know. All you gotta do is show me what's good, and then I got you. Come on, man. Open the door and let me handle my bitness. I got this."

I shook my head as if he could see me. "That's okay, Sharome. I just need a quick shower. I'll be out in a minute." I waited for his response, and when I didn't hear one, I assumed he got in the bed and went to sleep or left the house. Either way, in that moment I didn't care. I needed some relief, so I stepped into the shower, made sure the water was warm, closed my eyes, and took myself mentally to where I needed to be five times before I actually washed my body.

After I came out of the bathroom, I found Sharome had disappeared into the living room. I confirmed that as I looked down the hall and saw him sitting on the couch with his head bowed, our big screen television illuminating him. I wanted to go and try to talk about what had taken place, but I knew I didn't have the words he needed to hear. I understood I was his first and there was a lot he had to learn, but I didn't feel like I was suitable to teach him because I had some things going on inside me he would sure find strange, yet I couldn't help it. Shotgun had me so sexually awakened I didn't know what to do with myself. As much as I hated his guts, my body called out for all of the things he'd done to me.

But, instead of going into the living room that night, I casually crawled into the bed and got under the covers. Ten minutes later I was out like a light.

The next afternoon I was coming from having a meeting with the dean of admissions at N.Y.U. While walking down the hallway and reading a text on my phone from Shante, not looking where I was going, I ran into a man who was walking in the opposite direction. I almost fell on my ass, but he dropped his briefcase and wrapped his arms around me, catching me as I dropped my phone to the ground, shattering it.

"Are you okay, li'l lady?" he asked, holding me up and looking into my eyes with his light brown ones. He looked like a caramel-skinned version of Shemar Moore with more muscles. He smelled like Cool Water cologne, and I figured he was about forty years old. He brushed my hair out of my face making me blush.

I wiggled out if his embrace and reached down and picked up my phone, looking at the screen. It had a huge crack down the middle of it, and it was completely black. "I'm okay. I apologize for running into you. There's been some things going on in my family, and that was an important text I was reading."

He reached and picked up his briefcase. "Hey, don't mention it. In fact, let me apologize to you because I wasn't watching where I was going, either. Had I been, I would have wound up stopping you anyway. You're absolutely gorgeous. You have to allow me to take you out to lunch to make this up to you and pay for your phone to be fixed. It would be my joy. What do you say?"

I don't know why I did it or what I was thinking at the time, but somehow, some way we wound up sitting across from each other at Bertolli's. I'd ordered a Caesar salad with ranch dressing and had not eaten a bite. I couldn't take my eyes off of this older man. He was so handsome and welcoming. It seemed he had an endless array of compliments for me. Every time he finished with one, I found myself yearning for another.

He looked across the table and smiled. "So, are you a student at N.Y.U.?" He took a sip from his coffee, then looked at the face of his Rolex before pulling his sleeve back over it. He was dressed in a dark blue Roberto Cavili suit with a matching tie.

I shook my head. "Not yet, but hopefully soon. I met with the dean of admissions today. He seemed pretty optimistic I would be able to start in the fall if a few things fall together for me. Whatever that means." I picked up my lemonade and took a drink from it.

He smiled. "Well, I'm his divorce lawyer. He takes most of his advice from me, so if you need me to pull some strings for you, I'll be more than happy to do so. I feel like a woman as beautiful as you should be able to do anything you want and have everything you desire." He reached across the table and grabbed my hand, rubbing his thumb back and forth across it.

It took me a short while to pull it away. I felt so guilty when Sharome's face flashed into my mind. What made it so bad is the fact this man had me so taken that he'd told me his name twice and I still couldn't remember it. I was that enamored by him. "Thank you, uh?"

He laughed to himself. "Savan."

"Yeah, Savan. I'd really appreciate if you could help me out by whispering into the Dean's ear. You know, they have a really nice literary arts program I'd like to be a part of. I think somewhere down the line I'd like to write a few books. I mean,

I've already started a few, but want to acquire as many skills as possible. I'd like to see my name on the bestsellers list of the New York Times one day. That would be so cool." I smiled just imagining it.

Savan looked me over closely in silence, then took another sip from his coffee. "Well, I'll make sure you are able to take full advantage of that program. I'll take care of Dean Mathis, don't you worry. Now, in exchange for my assistance, what do you say you let me take you out to a nice dinner, and maybe a long limo ride around the city so I can continue to get to know you? There is something about you I find very intriguing, and almost familiar." He looked into my eyes, and I couldn't help blushing. I felt like a little schoolgirl who had a crush on her teacher.

I smiled. "I don't think there is any harm in a little dinner, though I will have to run it by my boyfriend. And to be honest, I don't know how he's going to take that." I imagined me telling Sharome I was going to have dinner with another man and saw him in my mind's eye snapping the hell out. I didn't know what I was going to tell him about Savan. I guess I would have to get my story straight before I said anything.

The waiter came to the table and set the bill down right in the middle of us. Before I could reach for it, Savan grabbed it and looked it over, then went into his pocket, taking out his wallet and setting down a crisp hundred-dollar bill.

"Hey, you don't have to do that. I'll pay for my own food. How much is my end of things?"

I reached for the bill that was encased in a little black folder, but Savan intercepted my hand, pulling it all the way to his mouth and kissing the back of it. His lips were soft and warm. He pressed them to my skin, and I think I even felt the tip of his tongue. "I could never be in your presence and allow you to pay for anything. You are that lovely. If you give me the chance to get to know you, you'll find out you and I have a lot in common."

Love Me Even When It Hurts 2

He reached and ran his fingers along the groove of my neck, and for some reason it stung just a tad. Then I remembered that while I'd been in the shower pleasing myself, I'd gotten a little rough while squeezing my neck. I'd broken the skin with a few of my nails by accident. I slowly moved his hand away, and I felt the tingles shooting all throughout my body. This man had some type of energy coming off him that was getting the better of me.

I avoided his eyes and cleared my throat, taking my Gucci purse and putting the strap over my shoulder. "Well, Savan, this has been nice. I have your card, and I look forward to reaching out to you in the very near future. I don't know about dinner. I'll have to get permission for that, but I hope that won't stop you from helping me with Dean Mathis?" I looked up at him. There were a few gray hairs in his beard that made him look even more sexy. In my opinion, it brought out his goatee even more.

He stood up and placed his arm outward. "Come on, I'll walk you to your car, and hopefully on the way I can convince you to take a risk and have dinner with me." He laughed and helped me out of my seat by taking my hand. I didn't think men were as polite and such gentlemen as he was.

We got outside of the restaurant. My car was parked across the street from his silver Range Rover truck. He walked me to his driver's side door, holding my hand the entire time. I was getting ready to release his hand when he pulled me to him and wrapped his arms around my lower back, looking down and into my eyes. Up that close I could smell his natural maleness. Once again it appealed to my womanly senses, and I felt so damn guilty. I didn't know what was wrong with me.

He leaned down and kissed me on the neck, right where the nails imprints were. First a gentle kiss, and then he licked them, causing me to shudder uncontrollably.

"Mm. I knew you'd taste good, Leesee. I pray you'll use my card soon. I promise to not get in the way of you and your boyfriend. I just want to show you a whole new side of life. A side I know you crave." He kissed my neck again, then sucked on it, pulling me closer to him.

I could feel his rock-hard chest against my small frame, and I felt dizzy. I tried to pry myself out of his grasp, but he held me firmly.

"Tell me you'll use it, baby girl. Promise me?"

He kissed my neck again, and now I could clearly feel my juices leaking out of me. Why did he have to call me baby girl? And why did hearing him call me that make me so wet? I started to shake. "I promise I'll be in touch, Savan. You have my word on that. Now I have to go or I'm going to be in some serious trouble." I loosened his arms from around me, shaking like I was freezing cold, then started to walk backward toward my car.

I don't know what I was thinking. All I know is I was shaking like crazy, barely able to keep my balance. I stepped backward about ten paces when I saw him look to his left. His eyes got big, and then he shot forward and snatched me out of the street and into the air. I wrapped my legs around him as we fell against the body of his truck.

To my right a car slammed on his brakes, and the white female driver got out of it in a frenzy. "Oh my god, I didn't see you! Are you okay?" she asked.

I had instinctively wrapped my legs around Savan. He held me in the air and brushed my hair out of my face. "You okay, Leesee?"

I nodded my head. "Yeah, I'm good. I don't know what I was thinking," I said, looking into his light brown eyes.

The white lady shook her head, then got back into her Chrysler and pulled away. I was still shaken up. Not from almost being hit by a car, but from the way Savan had snatched me up as if I were a rag doll.

Chapter 7

Leesee

I couldn't really remember how I got there, but the next thing I knew we were at Savan's penthouse, and he was throwing me up against the wall and sucking on my neck while taking my clothes off of me as if he couldn't wait for me to be naked. He kissed my lips and I kissed him back, breathing hard. My eyes were closed tight as I felt him pull up my skirt and slip his hand down my panties, rubbing my pussy in a circular motion, driving me nuts.

"I know what you need, Leesee. I can see it in your eyes. You need me to take this pussy. You yearn for it. Tell me?" He slid a finger up my kitty.

I arched my back and moaned out loud. "Uh! Please, Savan, don't do this. Uh, I'm begging you." I tried to push him away, then he turned me around, so I was facing the wall, pushed me into it and sucked on the back of my neck, licked up and down my spine before biting along the same path.

I shivered, then he dropped down and pushed my skirt up, yanking my panties down and off my ankles. I even lifted my feet one at a time so he could get them off. Then I felt him biting all over my ass cheeks before he smacked them and kissed the spot where he'd hit, then did the same to the other cheek before he sucked on one cheek after the next. "I'm going to conquer you, Leesee. I'm going to make you beg me to lay you down. Just watch." He stuffed his face in between my legs and began eating me out from the back while he flickered my clitoris back and forth. Then he'd pause and smacked my ass cheeks for a full minute, heating them up.

My legs were spread wide apart, my face against the wall, back arched in total submission to this man I'd just met. Sharome pushed himself into my mind, and I felt sick to my stomach. I didn't want to do him like this, but I needed this so bad. I needed Savan to take advantage of me. I needed to be used and conquered like he'd said. "Uh! Please, Savan!" I begged, though I didn't know what I was begging for because a part of me wanted him to stop, and an even bigger part wanted him to do whatever came to his mind.

He opened my butt cheeks and licked in between them, then pushed his tongue into my back door. I stood on my tippy-toes. It felt so good, but before I could get used to the feeling, he was slurping my sex lips into his mouth and attacking my clitoris. I began to shake and tremble. The sounds of his oral sex was driving me insane. It was so loud. I couldn't take it.

He slid two fingers up my box and got to working them in and out of me at full speed while he sucked on my jewel as if it were a chicken bone, pulling and nipping at it with his teeth like a vet, as if he knew my body to a T. Fuck, I loved older men. I had to admit that.

"'Uh! Uh! Uh!" I hollered, and then I was cumming hard. "Ah!" I fell forward into the wall while he feasted on my sex parts.

After I came, he stood up, got behind me, and grabbed a handful of my hair. My hard nipples rubbed against the wall as I felt his hot breath on my ear.

"Beg me for this dick, Leesee. Tell me you want it worse than your boyfriend's," he growled, then I felt his hard tool poking me in the butt. He ground it into my crack. I didn't even remember him pulling it out of his pants, but there it was, and it felt huge, hot, and throbbing against my backside. I wanted to cry out for it so bad. I needed him to slam it into me.

I guess I took too long to respond, because the next thing I knew he was picking me up and falling with me on his king size bed. I opened my legs as he got between them and wrapped his hand around my neck, squeezing. "Tell me you want me, Leesee. Beg me to take you right here and right now. Do it!"

He squeezed even tighter, and my kitty started to drool my essence. I gagged and struggled to breathe, humping up into him, needing to feel some part of him against my clit. I was dying with hunger for him. "Ack! Ack! I need! Ack! Need you," was all I managed to get out.

He flipped me over to my stomach and pushed my face into the sheets. Taking a handful of my hair, he forced my face further into the bed. "Stay just like that. Keep that ass in the air, and don't move. Submit to me," he growled.

I felt him getting out of the bed. I stayed just like he left me, with my ass in the air and my kitty on full display.

Seconds later he returned and got back behind me, grabbed my hair, then *smack*! I felt the blow slam into my ass cheek. It sent ripples all throughout my body. I yelped and closed my eyes as more and more blows came, each one causing me to become wetter and wetter. Then he was rubbing my kat, fingering me at full speed before attacking my cheeks again. "Beg me, Leesee! Beg me!"

"Fuck me, Savan! Please! Fuck me right now! I need you so bad!" I cried, not caring what I sounded like. I needed his body in the roughest way possible. He smacked me on the ass again with force. I yelped and spread my legs further apart. I needed him to touch me so bad. "Please!" I begged as he grabbed a handful of my hair again and stuffed my face into the bed.

Then I felt him get behind me. I could hear the sounds of plastic, there was some fumbling behind me, then I felt him slowly entering my womb while he pulled my hair, so my back arched.

"This my pussy from here on out. You don't never turn me down, do you hear me, Leesee? Tell me you understand!" he hollered and slammed into me with a vengeance, fucking me harder than I had ever been fucked before. His piece felt like it had to be every bit of eleven inches because Sharome was well endowed, and even he had not hit the spots Savan was hitting on every stroke. I felt like I couldn't even breathe.

"Uh, uh, uh, uh, huh, uh. I. Savan. Mm. Daddy! I. I. I. Ooh!" I moaned, bouncing back into him, trying my best to not think about how I was betraying my man.

He yanked my head backward by my hair, treating me like I needed to be treated. "Tell me this pussy is mine, Leesee! Tell me. I'm not gon' ask you again," he said through rugged breaths, only able to pronounce one word at a time. He sped up his pace and started to really dig me out.

"Ah!" I screamed, cumming all over him. "It's. It's. It's. It's yours, Savan. It's. It's. It's yours! Ooh!" I hollered, and then another ripple hit me.

He flipped me over onto my back and started to choke me while he fucked me so hard, I started to cry. It felt so good I didn't know what to do.

"Yeah. Yeah, I knew when I first saw you that. That. That. Ooh! You just like me! Mm, this pussy good! Shit!" he hollered, leaning down and sucking my hard, right nipple into his mouth while his hips rolled, plunging his dick deep into my lower abdomen.

He pushed my knees to my chest and got to screwing me so fast and hard I passed out twice and came back as I was cumming each time. The romp ended with him laying back and forcing me to suck him while he slapped my ass cheeks and told me how I belonged to him from there on out.

I was just getting out of the tub with a towel wrapped around me when Sharome came into the house, followed by Tia. I was so exhausted that even though I wanted to question how they'd managed to link up, I didn't even have to energy to argue with either one of them. I heard Tia making her way up the stairs to her portion of the house and Sharome making his way down the long hallway. The closer he got, the more guilty I felt until I thought I was going to start crying.

"Yo, Leesee. Baby, you woke in there?" he asked, halfway down the hall.

Love Me Even When It Hurts 2

I hurried and dropped the bath towel, slipping into my pink boyshorts. "Yeah, babe, I'm in here," I said, throwing my tank top over my head and situating my breasts inside of it.

He walked into the room carrying a bag. As soon as he saw me, he tossed it on the bed and came all the way around it and snatched me into his embrace, kissing my lips that were still a li'l sore from Savan sucking and biting all over them. I winced in pain but tried my best to fight through as to not bring attention to the problem.

"Damn, I been missing you all day. Every time I blinked my eyes, I was seeing your face. I'm sorry about last night. I wanna make that up to you, if you'll allow me to." He looked into my eyes with his gray ones.

I held his stare for a brief moment, then I looked off. I felt so dirty within his arms. I hated myself for doing what I'd just done less than two hours ago. I'd betrayed the only man who really cared about me, and I wanted to die in that moment.

He kissed me again, then backed away. "You ain't gotta forgive me just yet, but I hope you will when you see these." He reached into the bag and came up with a Kay's jewelry box and handed it to me. "That's for you, and I got a few other things in here, too. Just some things I felt you should have. Nah mean?"

I felt a lump form in my throat, then my stomach turned upside down as if I was going to throw up. I didn't deserve whatever was in that box. I didn't deserve him. I didn't deserve to be loved in the fashion he loved me. I hated myself so bad.

"Baby, I already forgive you. It's okay. Like I said, I just wanted to try some things with you, that's all."

He shook his head. "Nah, but I came at you all wrong. I was hollering at Tia, and she was saying plenty women ain't with that boring-ass sex like most niggaz used to putting down. It gotta be spicy. I just didn't know that 'cause you ain't never tell me. But now I do. You know you my first piece of monkey, so I'ma rookie to all of that, but I'm willing to learn.

Jelissa

Word is bond, I'll do anything for you, Leesee. You should know that."

Now I was crying, and I felt even worse than a few moments before. I sat on the bed as snot leaked out of my nose. I wiped it away and opened the box slowly, nearly losing my breath. I covered my mouth with my hand.

"Yo, that's a pink-faced Rollie. They just released that kind a day ago. I know them rapper chicks always talking about Rolexes and stuff, and it seems like it's all the craze now, so I had to make sure my baby had her own when you roll up into N.Y.U. I can't allow for nobody to shine harder than my woman. I also got you this." He went into the bag and pulled out a quarter-length Eve St. Laurent black-and-white leather jacket and handed it to me, along with a new iPhone.

I dropped my head into my lap and stared crying like a baby.

He ran around and wrapped his arms around my neck. "What's the matter, Leesee? I thought you'd be happy, baby. I hope I ain't offended you. I just wanted to apologize for last night. I don't like when you're mad at me, I can't handle that, baby. You're my everything. I swear you are." He kissed my cheek and knelt down in front of me.

I closed the box and threw it on the bed. "Why do you love me so much, Sharome? I don't deserve it. I'm not right. You're not supposed to love me this hard. Nobody is," I whimpered before crying my heart out loudly. I fell to my knees beside him and lowered my face to the floor. Scenes from hours ago replaying themselves in my mind. I felt sicker and sicker.

He pulled me to him and kissed my forehead. "You deserve more love than I can offer you. I need you to know that. You're my absolute everything, Leesee. I'll give my life for you. You're all that matters in this world to me."

I shook my head as I cried into his chest. I wanted to tell him I shouldn't mean so much, that I was nothing more than trash, and he should have seen me as such. I was damaged

72

goods. The calling between my legs would forever run my life, I felt. I needed him to love me, but not so much because I felt that deep down I was going to hurt him one way or the other. It was just in me.

He held me tighter. "You're my angel, baby. You're so special, and I'm going to die trying to give you the world."

He held me for the next hour, telling me how much I meant to him and how he was never going to leave my side. With every word of validation of his love, I felt weaker and weaker to the point I was about to throw up. Luckily it stayed down, and we wound up falling asleep on the floor together with me wrapped in his big arms of muscle.

The next morning, he brought me breakfast in bed, then sat at the foot of the bed and rubbed my feet, taking time out to kiss each individual toe. "You're so perfect baby. I'm so glad you're my woman. I mean that with all of my heart."

Tia came down the stairs and knocked on our bedroom door. I swallowed the food I had in my mouth and took a sip of Apple juice before I asked who was at our door.

"It's Tia. Can I come in?" she asked.

I rolled my eyes. "Yeah, girl, come in."

She opened the door and poked her head inside. "Everybody dressed, right?" She stepped into the room wearing some tight, black biker shorts and a black sports bra that did little to stop her hard nipples from poking through the fabric.

Sharome kissed my toes again, then rubbed his cheek against them. "Yeah, we good, but I still ain't had the chance to run everything by her as of yet." He sat my feet down and sat beside me, wiping the corner of my mouth on a napkin.

I raised an eyebrow. "Run what by me?" I sat up and looked from him to her, then back to him again. "What, Sharome?"

He exhaled loudly. "Nah, look, yo' cousin trying to get her bands up, and I'm willing to help her.

Jelissa

I scrunched my face and mugged the shit out of Tia. I felt like that bitch was always up to something. Now my man was talking about putting some money in her pocket. I wasn't wit' that shit. I didn't give a fuck what plan they'd come up wit'.

"Damn, Leesee, don't snap out before you even know what's good," Tia said, frowning.

I was seconds away from getting out of my bed and fucking her up. I was sick of her acting like she was entitled to Sharome or something. That was getting to me like I can't even explain.

"Well, somebody better tell me somethin', and fast. And fuck what you talkin' about, Tia, fo' real, because I don't like you and my man discussing shit behind my back. I should be the first to know. I should know everything he doin' or plannin' before you, every single time, not the other way around. Me and you gon' have some problems if you don't stay in yo' lane when it comes to him. I know you my big cousin and all, but that ain't gon' stop me from fucking you up Jersey-style. Keep trying me." I felt my heartbeat speed up. "Now, what's good?" I mugged Sharome.

Tia sucked her teeth and crossed her arms over her chest.

He shook his head. "Like I was saying, Tia trying to get her bands up, and I wanna help her. You see, I'm finna be trafficking some heavy work back and forth from here to South Beach, and I need a female driver with an I.D. and insurance. Since I don't know or trust none of these females out this way, and I definitely ain't letting you get involved, I felt like she was the safest choice. Plus, that way the money would stay in the crib, and it'll help her get on her feet. She one hunnit as far as I can see. Plus, I wanna make sure she just as good before she bounce from the crib. This gig gon' pay her seven gees a pop," he said, rubbing my naked thighs over the cover.

I curled my lip. "You just wanna look out for her, huh? Yeah, I bet you do. When all this supposed to go down, and for how long?" I asked, looking from one of them to the other.

Love Me Even When It Hurts 2

Sharome rolled his head around on his neck. "It starts tomorrow, and as far as when it stops, I don't know just yet. I guess we gon' get it while the getting is good."

"Look, Leesee, if you ain't cool wit' it, I ain't gon' sweat it. I was just trying to find a way to get right, that's all. I been around this shit my whole life, so I know what's good. I'd make sure I watched his back to the best of my abilities, whereas if he tried and had another chick do the job, she could potentially set his ass up somewhere down the road. You already know how grimy these hoez are out here." She ran her tongue across her teeth and placed her hand on her hip.

I looked at her like she was crazy. "Bitch, that's what they said you did to a nigga out in Brooklyn." I blew air through my teeth and shook my head.

She opened her mouth wide and looked as if she were shocked I'd even brought that up.

"Am I right, though?"

She rolled her eyes and stormed out of the room. "I ain't got time for this shit, Leesee. I don't know what's gotten into you. Sharome, let me know what's good when you come out of there." She closed the door behind her, continuing to talk to herself as she made her way down the hallway.

Sharome stood up and pulled out a knot of cash. "The only way we gon' keep on seeing figures like this is if you let that girl be my driver. If not her, then it's gon' be some other broad, and I know you ain't having that." He went into the closet and moved all of his shoeboxes out of the way before moving the wall so he could slide his mini-refrigerator-sized safe out of it. The machine beeped as he entered in his passcode.

"Yo, how much paper you got on you right now? Do you need a gee or somethin'?" he asked, hollering with his face in the safe.

I got out of the bed and pulled my tank top down over my stomach because the room felt a li'l chilly. "I'm good. And I don't give a fuck if she drives for you, Sharome. I just don't

75

like y'all making plans behind my back. I feel like I'm being left out of everything when I'm supposed to be your woman."

He finished messing around with the safe, then put everything back the way it had been at first. Then he stood in front of me, looking all handsome, taking my hands into his. "Baby, I'd never leave you out in the cold. I love you way too much for that. I'm honestly just trying to figure some things out to make sure you never have need for anything. You know I'm your sacrifice. I always will be."

I shook my head, then laid it on his chest. "Damn, I'm tripping again, Sharome. I know you mean well. Handle yo' bidness, baby. Whatever you need to do to make things happen for us, you have my full blessing. I trust you one hunnit percent." I looked up and he kissed me on my lips, reaching around and cuffing my booty cheeks roughly. They were still tender from all of Savan's sucking and manhandling of them. I felt so guilty for cheating on Sharome, and the worst part was I didn't know if it was going to happen again.

Chapter 8

Rome

I felt the sweat beading on my forehead as I jumped out of the Lexus truck and went to open the door to the back so I could grab both big, black duffle bags. It was three in the afternoon on a hot Miami evening, and I found myself pulling into the garage of a sanitation company where I was met by five heavily-armed Haitians with half of their faces covered with black bandanas. They lowered their eyes into slits as I got out of the truck to retrieve their merchandise. This was my first drop-off to them, and I couldn't lie and say I wasn't worried out of my mind. I felt at any moment somethin' bad was about to happen. I could feel the sweat pouring all down my back.

As soon as the doors to the back of the truck where opened, one of the gunmen approached me with his assault rifle aimed at my chest. I threw my hands up. "Yo, what's this all about, homeboy?" I asked, ready to up my .40 caliber out of my waistband and try my luck, though I knew from the looks of things it would have been a losing battle.

He grabbed my shirt and threw me backward into the truck, then turned me around and started to search me. While he was doing this, Tia was snatched out of the truck and threw up against it alongside me so she could go through the same procedure.

"This ain't nothin' personal, Rude Boy. Juss me first time seein' you iz all. Wanna make sure itz all good," he said, running his hands all over me, making me feel so uncomfortable. Then he located my .40 caliber and took it off my waist, handing it to one of his goons.

I looked to my right and saw the way the dude was running his hands up and down Tia's body, and it pissed me off. "Say,

Jelissa

nigga, get yo' muthafuckin' hands off her. She ain't got shit. She just my approved driver, per Sycleff," I hollered.

The goon's eyes lowered, but he kept on feeling all over her ass, and I lost it. I pushed backward into the Haitian who was searching me, knocking him away, then I rushed over to the dude searching Tia, cocked back, and punched him right in the jaw with all of my might, knocking his ass out cold. Then I stood in front of her, making sure she was securely behind me. All of the guns in the place were pointed at us. The one I'd knocked out lay on his side, unmoving.

"Now, we here to do bidness. Y'all can get off all of this fuck-shit, word is bond."

The dude who had been searching me stepped into my face and placed his forehead almost to mine. "You got heart, Rude Boy. Ya fire off on a man in my army and not worry about the consequences. I like that. I'll be sure to let Sycleff know you got balls as big as a donkey's. Go and get me the merch."

I looked him in the eyes and nodded my head, then turned my back to him. "Tia, get in the truck and lock the door. We almost up out of here." I lead her to the truck and opened the door for her while I mugged the shooters. I didn't like these niggaz. They just rubbed me the wrong way. I knew they were cold-hearted killas because Ramsey had warned me, but I didn't give a fuck. I wasn't finna sit back and allow Tia to be assaulted by none of them predator-ass niggaz. I'd rather die first.

I snatched the duffle bags out of the truck and sat them at his feet. He knelt down with a pocketknife, unzipped the bag, and pulled out a wrapped package. He stabbed it and tasting the contents on his knife, nodding his head as he looked at me with his gray eyes, like my own. Then he stood up and waved for a man to come to him.

The dude turned his back to us, reached into a big dumpster, and came up with two black duffle bags that looked a lot like the ones I'd brought with me. He walked all the way over to us and placed them at my feet. "That's 250 kilos of

78

pure Sycleff. He sends his wishes to your boss. We'll see you soon." He knelt down and picked up the man I'd knocked out.

I mugged his bitch-ass before grabbing my gun back from the first dude who'd searched me, placing the bags into the back of the truck and leaving their property.

Ramsey said whenever we made moves, no matter what, we weren't supposed to hit the roads after six at night. I was calculating the time in my head, and I knew there was no way we'd make it back to New York before that time, so I checked us into the Hyatt where we'd spend the night, hitting the road first thing in the morning.

Tia waited until the door closed before she walked up to me and wrapped her arms around my neck, laying her head on my chest. I dropped both duffle bags and held her for a minute. I could hear her sniffling as if she were crying.

"What's the matter, Tia? I hope it ain't that shit from back there wit' them Haitian niggaz," I said, feeling myself become heated. No woman should've had to go through what she just did. I wanted to kill that predator-ass dude. My heart was heavy for her. I felt like I'd failed in protecting her.

She looked up at me with tears in her eyes, trailing down her cheeks and dripping off her chin. "I been in the projects and around hustlers my whole life, and ain't none of them ever stepped up for me the way you just did. Them studs could have killed you back there, and you didn't even care. You wasn't about to let the dude take advantage of me, and that's all there was to it. I don't know why you stepped up, but I thank you for doing it, Sharome." She stepped on her tippy-toes and kissed my cheek, then started to rub the back of my neck with her face in my chest. She popped back on her legs, and I saw that ass jiggle while looking over her shoulder.

"Yo, it's good, Tia. I ain't about to let nobody hurt you like that. You risin' wit' me, and we gotta have each other's backs, especially while we're doing this shit. You need to know I got you, and I need to know the same thing. Nah

Jelissa

mean?" I rubbed her back and trailed my hands down to her waist, holding it in my hands. I could smell her perfume.

She looked up at me and into my eyes, sucking on her bottom lip before standing on her tippy-toes and lightly pecking me on the lips.

I jerked my head backward and released our hold. "Yo, we gotta chill on that, though, shorty. We can't fuck around and get ourselves in trouble, and I love Leesee too much for that. You feel me?"

She smiled and nodded her head. "I hear you, and I ain't trying to go there wit' you, but a kiss is only a kiss. Ain't no harm in that, so don't make it weird." She stepped back into my face and kissed me again, this time with a little more conviction.

I held her small waist, and without even thinking about it trailed my hands down until they were cupping her ass cheeks. As soon as she moaned into my mouth, my brain caught up with my penis and I broke our kiss, wiping my mouth and feeling like I'd just murdered Leesee in cold blood. "Yo, let's chill out, Tia. Fo' real, I can't get down like that. I love my girl with all my heart. I can't do her like that. That ain't one hunnit."

She lowered her head and took a step back. "Okay, you're right. I was bogus for that. Let me go take a cool shower, and then maybe we can order some room service and lean back and watch a movie. Can you at least hold me? Is that cool. I mean, since we family and all?" she asked, raising her right eyebrow.

I laughed. "Yeah, that's cool, just as long as we keep shit on the up-and-up. I don't see no problem wit' that."

She sucked her bottom lip into her mouth, looking so bad I had to look at the floor because I was feeling some type of way. "I'll be good. And hey, since we watching a movie, why don't you order Fifty Shades Freed and it'll show you what Leesee was talking about. That cool?" she asked, turning to face the bathroom, but looking at me over her shoulder.

My eyes went down to her round ass, and I couldn't help looking it over. It was so round and plump, just like Leesee's. I don't know why I was jocking hers when I had one the same size at home, but unfortunately, I was, and it was making me feel some type of way.

"Yeah, that's cool. I'll order us a bottle and get everything set up."

I should have known I was in trouble when she came out of the bathroom in just her pink-and-black, tight boyshorts and a pink-laced Victoria's Secret Pink collection matching bra. The material was made so I could make out both of her nipples as clear as day. Her flat stomach looked like it needed to be kissed all over. I could do nothin' but take a deep breath as she climbed into the bed and lay her head on my chest.

I'd removed my Michael Kors shirt and bulletproof vest and was only donned in a tight, black wife beater. She rubbed her hand up and down my stomach, lying on her side. The boyshorts conformed to her ass, leaving very little to the imagination.

"You got the movie ready to go?" she asked, looking up at me.

I looked into her eyes and felt a weird-ass, forbidden spark. I had to shake it off immediately. Something was telling me to get the fuck out of that bed, and I think she must've sensed it because the next thing she did was wrap her right leg over me.

"G'on 'head and start it, then pass me that Ace of Spades."

Everything was cool for a little while. We were watching the movie and eating the pizza I'd ordered for us to snack on while we sipped the bottle of Ace. She was being one hunnit and keeping shit on the up-and-up until the real heavy sex scenes got to playing in the movie. Then she got to grinding into my hip and breathing all heavy, laying her head on me chest before snaking her hand under my shirt so she could rub all over my naked abs.

Jelissa

"Mm, ain't this shit turning you on, Sharome? Can't you see why she want you to do this type of shit to her?" she whispered before placing her cheek against mine and rubbing it up and down.

I couldn't lie, the movie had my dick rock hard and throbbing. It was so hard it hurt. I had to get my ass up out of that bed. I was feeling some type of way. "Yeah, this boy is lit," I said, trying to find a strategic way to get up out of that bed so I could go and take a walk. I needed some fresh air.

Tia ran her hand all over my stomach, then brought it down to my waistband, and before I could stop her, she was in my boxers, squeezing my hard dick in her hand.

I groaned, reached down, and pulled her hand off of me, and tried to sit up. "Yo, I need to take a walk. Yo' li'l ass gon' get me in trouble." I made a move to get out of the bed.

She straddled my lap and forced me back onto the bed. "Nall, Sharome. Damn, we grown as hell. I'll let you tie me up right now, and you can do anything to me. I mean anything. I just wanna feel you inside of me, the long way. I need to show you how she wants you to put it down for her. Trust me, she'll thank me later." She leaned down and bit into my neck hard, sucking it like a vampire. Sliding her hand between our bodies and into my boxers again, she took ahold of my piece. Her wet lips made a lot of noise as she kissed all over my neck. "Let me teach you, baby. Let me show you how this shit go, or you gon' lose Leesee. Trust me." She bit into my neck again.

I groaned out loud, reached down and grabbed her big ass, massaging the globes while she moaned with her mouth open.

"Yes, yes, Sharome. Let's do this. I promise you'll thank me in the end."

The next thing I knew she had my wrists tied to the headboard so tight they hurt. I tired to see if I could free them, and I couldn't. She straddled me and ran her nails down my chest, scratching, then biting my skin with her teeth.

82

"I'm gon' show you, Sharome. Let me teach you how to use this big-ass dick. It's worthless unless you know what's good."

She sucked it into her mouth and got to giving me the best head of my life with no hands, her mouth full of spit. The harder she sucked, the louder the noises that came from her mouth and my pipe. Even though it was feeling good, I was starting to have remorse. I couldn't do Leesee like that. Not with her cousin. Not with anybody. I struggled to free my hands from the bonds, but she had them tied tight.

Up and down her mouth went, pushing me closer and closer to the point of no return. She popped me out of her mouth with a loud *thwack* sound. "Cum in my mouth, Sharome. It's good. You can cum in it. I owe you that for standing up for me." She slurped me back into her mouth and got to pumping me at full speed. She dug her nails into my thighs, adding to the pleasure, and groaned all over it. "Mm! Mm! Mm!"

I struggled against the bonds as my toes curled. Leesee's beautiful face popped into my head. I got to imagining it was her sucking me with so much precision. I saw her naked body in my mind, the way she walked, her touch, and then I rose my hips up off of the bed and came with all of my might.

"Aw! Shit!" I hollered.

Tia wrapped her hand around my throat and squeezed while she stroked my penis up and down. More and more of my fluids spilled out of me. The feel of her hand around my neck sent me on a journey.

"That's what she wanna feel, Sharome. She needs this kind of shit. You gotta make it hurt to make it feel good." She leaned down and bit my chest while she stroked me at full speed. Then she straddled me and climbed my body, placing her naked pussy over my mouth, humping my face. "Taste me now. Taste this chocolate pussy and tell me if we taste alike. Mm! Shit, baby!"

Jelissa

She opened her lips and forced them up against my mouth. I turned my head from right to left to avoid the inevitable, then she slapped the shit out of me and held my face. "Eat this pussy, Sharome. I'm not asking you no more, nigga! I'm telling you to!" Them she opened her thighs wider and humped into my face while she held the top of the headboard.

I don't know why I did it, or why I didn't try harder to not do it, but the next thing I knew I was licking up and down her slit, sucking on her sex lips and wanting her to force me to do something else I didn't want to do. I closed my eyes and once again imagined she was Leesee, forcing me to eat her pussy, taking all of my power away from me, taking charge. And I liked it because I knew I would do anything for her. I'd break my neck to submit to Leesee any day of the week. She was my everything.

Tia continued to hump into my face, holding her sex lips way apart. Every time I opened my eyes I was looking directly at her inner pinkness, and it drove me crazy.

"Mm, yes! Yes! Yes! Sharome, just like that, baby. Eat this pussy. Submit to me. I run this shit. Me. Little ol' me. Bow down! Uh!" She screamed and tossed her head backward.

I sucked and licked and sucked some more, trapping her wet clit with my lips and trying to pull it from the top of her slit. With every nip of it she'd scream at the top of her lungs, grab my head, and hump into me faster and faster. Her juices dripped off my chin and ran down my neck, along the path of my upper chest. The more she pushed my face into her, the more excited I became until I needed her to touch me.

"Uh! I'm cumming, Sharome! I'm cumming all over yo' pretty face, baby. Ooh, it's so good! It's so, so good! Huh!" She humped faster and faster, knocking my head into the headboard again and again until she collapsed on the side of me, shaking as if she were having a seizure.

I lay on my back with my chest heaving up and down. My piece continued to jerk up and down, throbbing, begging for

84

some action. "Tia? Tia? Let me out of these bonds, man, fo' real," I said. I needed to get to the bathroom so I could pleasure myself, because the more my penis jerked, I got to looking at her body, and I was seconds away from asking her to jump on my tool and ride me like she hated my guts. But I couldn't do Leesee like that. I had already gone far enough.

Tia moaned and bit into her bottom lip, got on her knees, and turned all the way around so her ass was facing me, and her head was close to my pipe. She leaned down and blew on the head, sending shivers all throughout me. "Mm, look at this big-ass dick. You want me to sit on it for you, baby?" She rubbed it against her cheek and spread her thighs farther apart. I couldn't help looking at her wet sex lips. They were chocolate and slightly open, just enough for me to see a hint of her rose. Her scent was all feminine, and it was giving me a hard time. I wanted that pussy in that moment. I was going through so many mixed emotions. I didn't know what to do.

I struggled against the bonds again. "Nall, I'm good, Tia. Just let me go. We done went far enough."

She reached under herself and spread her pussy lips, looking over her shoulder at me as she lay her face on the bed. "You sure you don't want none of this kitty? I promise you it'll change yo' life. Word is bond." She ran her middle finger back and forth across her clit, then got up and crawled until she placed my penis up against her sex lips from the back. Once there she moved it up and down her slit. "Uh! Shit. Tell me you don't wanna hit this pussy. Tell me, Sharome." She backed into me, took my dick head, and put it into her hole a little bit, then pulled it back out. Her heat felt so good. It felt like a soft, velvet oven. I wanted it so bad.

"Nall, man, I'm good. Mm. stop playing, Tia, and take me out of this shit." I bit into my bottom lip and watched as her ass opened up and slightly jiggled every time she moved. In my opinion there was nothing like a big booty on a sista, and hers was all project booty. I was yearning for it, but I had to maintain my composure. I couldn't fuck over Leesee like that, even though it was so hard not to.

Tia turned all the way around and straddled me, then reached behind her and placed my dick head right on her opening before sliding down it. Her heat suffocated me, and the walls squeezed me so tight I felt like I couldn't breathe. Then I noticed I was holding my breath.

"See, you ain't never had no stripper pussy before. It's a reason why hoez don't want us around their men, and you finna find out, but first you gon' beg me to fuck you like I'm supposed to. Beg me to ride this dick, Sharome. Now!" She grabbed my neck and slammed my head backward into the headboard.

I felt a spark go off in me, and I began to shake like crazy. Here was this woman, no more than five feet, two inches tall, dominating me like I was smaller than her. That shit was so hot to me. She rose all the way up and fell back down on my dick again. I could feel her walls squeezing me off and on.

Once my dick was fully implanting into her, she humped forward and dug her nails into my throat. "You want me. I need to hear it."

At this point I was so gone I refused to think about what we were finna do. I just needed some relief, and her pussy felt so damn good. That heat was amazing. She slid up my piece again, then fell down it, squeezing my neck, and that was all she wrote. I threw all caution to the wind. "Fuck me, Tia! Hurry up and handle yo' bidness, man, please. Shit!" I hollered, humping into her, trying to go as deep as I possibly could.

She leaned forward and licked the left side of my face, sucking on my neck with force. "That's the shit I'm talking 'bout. Now watch me do my thing. I guarantee you gon' be fien'ing for this pussy from here on out, and the thing is anytime you want it, you can have it. But you gon' have to beg me for it. And don't worry, I can keep a secret."

Love Me Even When It Hurts 2

She rose and fell down, and every time she implanted herself on my piece, she'd roll her hips and bite me in a new place. That night she rode me for two hours straight and made me beg her to keep going. My dick had never stayed hard for so long. I think it was because she handled me so rough. The way she talked to me and put down her sex game had me mentally shook. I didn't know what I was going to do now that I had betrayed my woman by sleeping with her cousin. I felt so damn lost after Tia untied my hands and crawled on top of me, looking into my eyes.

"Look, Sharome, don't feel no type of way. It's good. I ain't gon' say shit to my cousin." She kissed my chest and rubbed all over my abs. "I don't mind being the side chick because you always keep me straight anyway. I feel like I owe you this pussy, so let's just keep looking out for each other and not make a big deal of things. No harm, no foul." She kissed my lips, then hopped off of me. "I enjoyed it. You got some good dick on you. I definitely ain't about to say shit."

She blew me a kiss, then I watched her walk into the bathroom naked. Her brown ass cheeks jiggled on her frame, along with her thick thighs. The entire room smelled like our rumble in the bed. All the images were going through my head, and I was starting to feel sick to my stomach. How could I have betrayed my lady like that? I felt like a straight sucka, fo' real.

"Order us some breakfast before we hit the road, Sharome. I'm hungry as hell!" she hollered from the bathroom, and I could tell she didn't have a care in the world.

I felt sick.

Jelissa

Chapter 9

Shotgun

"Let me go, Shotgun. I'm tired of this shit! You don't let me do nothin'. I don't wanna be that bitch no more. I wanna be myself. I wanna–"

Smack!

"Ugh!"

Smack!

Tracy fell to the floor. I knelt down and picked her up by her hair. There was a trickle of blood in the corner of her mouth. I took my thumb and wiped it up, then sucked it off. It tasted like a copper penny. "Bitch, you gon' be Leesee until I say you ain't. You forget I own you. You're my muthafuckin' property, and when it's time for me to dismiss yo' ass, you best believe I will in the way I want to, you got that?" I smacked her again with all of my might and slung her pretty ass to the floor.

It had only been three months since I'd taken her from Simone, and already she was beginning to become too lippy for my taste. "Clean up this muthafuckin' house, and I'll be back when I'm back. I'm setting this alarm, so if you open any window or door around this muthafucka I'ma have every police in Newark on yo' ass. They gon' deliver you back to me, and when they do, bitch, I'ma cut yo' throat out and throw it in yo' lap. That's my word."

She crawled into a corner of the living room holding her face, sitting with her back against the wall, looking up at me and trembling as if she was freezing cold. "I swear to God; I hate you so much. I wish you'da left me wit' Simone. All you do is hurt me, Shotgun. One day you gon' get yours. One day somebody gon' get yo' ass back for how you do people!" she screamed in anger.

Jelissa

I laughed at her stupid ass, set the security system, and left the house after slamming the door. I ain't have time for that bullshit. I needed somethin' new, anyway. Tracy was starting to get on my last nerve.

As I stepped onto the porch, I was met by the harsh rays of the sun beaming down on me as if nature had somethin' against me. I'd not been on the porch more than two minutes when I began to sweat. It was humid, and I could tell wearing the bulletproof vest was going to be uncomfortable.

I jumped into my black Charger and was stung by the leather seats the sun had heated up. Reaching forward after closing my driver's side door, I flipped on the air conditioner, took a deep breath, then tried to gather my thoughts. My mind was all over the place. The voices seemed as if they were all around me, and had I really listened to my psychiatrist, I would have sworn up and down my schizophrenia was getting worse. That and my mood continued to be up one minute, then extremely low in the next. I was missing my baby girl, Leesee, like crazy and was pissed off that Capo had not held up his end of things. I felt it was time to pay him a visit.

Ten minutes later I pulled up to Vino's carwash and parked my car in the parking lot, slamming the door and chirping the alarm. I noted that Capo's men were busy at work. The parking lot was full of cars waiting to be serviced or washed. Loud music from a few of the car's radios blared, along with the vacuum cleaners. As I walked toward the business, I caught the eye of a few beautiful women that licked their lips and smiled, obviously on the prowl and looking for the next mark that would pay all of their bills. I wasn't going. That trick shit had never been in my blood. I dismissed them with an upturn of my nose and made my way inside.

Old man Vino was sitting behind the desk, listening to his radio that played a nice old tune from the Temptations. As soon as he saw me, his eyes got big as paper plates. He cleared his throat and pulled his collar away from his neck. "Shotgun, what brings you here, man? It ain't time for yo' payment already, is it?" he asked, picking up a white Styrofoam cup and sipping out of it.

I shook my head. "Let me in the back. I know Capo back there, and we got some bidness to attend to. Call him and let him know I'm here."

I looked over my shoulder as a short, redbone sista dressed in a tight, red mini-skirt showcasing her thick thighs and ample bottom stepped past me and looked over the counter at Vino.

"Dad, do you think you can have them get my car done and out the way? I have an hour before I have to be at my first photo shoot." She popped back on her legs and whipped her hair over her shoulders.

Damn, I was mesmerized.

Vino, an old, dark-skinned dude with a bald head and gray beard, nodded his head. "Yeah, baby, just give me one second. Let me get him squared away." He picked up the phone and I assumed called to the back to alert Capo I was present. After hanging up the phone, he turned back to me and lifted the divider so I could step past him and into the door directly behind him. It led to a short hallway that had two doors. One was a bathroom, and the other the manager's office.

Before I went, I looked to my right at the fine specimen of a woman and still couldn't believe how fine she was. "Say, Ms. Lady, this man right here is your biological father?" I asked, disbelieving.

She turned to look at me, running her tongue across her teeth then popping her lips. The nipples on her B-cup breasts were hard and poking through her white-and-red Fendi top. "Yeah. Why do you ask me that?"

"Please, he's waiting for you back there, Shotgun. It's best you go now," Vino said nervously. I could tell he was worried.

I laughed at that and looked over his daughter. She couldn't have been more than eighteen, if that. I sucked my lips loudly and looked her up and down, then over her shoulder at her red Lexus, memorizing the plates. I'd look her

Jelissa

up later. "Oh, no reason. I just wanted to know. I'm sure I'll see you again, li'l lady. Until then, you take care of yourself, and be thankful you didn't grow up to look like him," I joked, though I was serious as hell. Her old man was ugly as a gorilla.

I took a step back and looked at that fat-ass booty, shook my head, then made my way into the back of the business after hearing her giggle. Yeah, she had to be young, I figured. In the background I could hear Vino chastising her.

I stepped up to the office door, and before I could knock the door opened. I was met with the face of Kazi. He curled his upper lip and mugged me with hatred. I guessed he was still holding a grudge for what I'd done to his mother. I didn't give a fuck. In my mind she was supposed to die because of the daughter she'd allowed her son to take away from me. I stepped into Kazi's face and pressed my forehead against his. "Fuck you looking at me like that for, homeboy?"

He swallowed, took his pistol off of his waist, and cocked it after taking a step back. "Word is bond, I'll smoke yo' bitch-ass, Shotgun. You betta check yo'self, cuz. All that fuck-shit ain't gon' keep flying, ma nigga." He scrunched his face, and I noticed his trigger finger constantly moving.

I pulled out my Glock .40, cocked it, and aimed the gun at his forehead, pressing the barrel against his skin. "Who the fuck you think you talking to, li'l nigga? Huh? Nigga, I know you ain't 'bout that life. If you was, I'd be dead already, but I ain't cuz you's a bitch-nigga!" I pushed his head backward with the gun. "Now sit yo' simple ass down before I smoke you like I did yo' pops. Soft-ass nigga!"

I felt my heart pounding in my chest. My vision was starting to go hazy, and my mouth was filling up with saliva. All of those things usually happened at one time when I was getting ready to kill somethin'.

Kazi lowered his head and looked at the floor with a crazy look on his face. I could tell he was trying his best to not flip out. I knew the young nigga was a killa, but I refused to allow him to piss on my gangsta. I didn't give a fuck if I was the police or not. I was Shotgun before anythang.

Capo stood up and held a hand in the air. "Come on, now, fellas. We ain't got time for all of that. It's all love in this room. Nah mean?" He looked from Kazi to me. "Shotgun, I still got my hittas out there scouring the whole east coast to find yo' daughter and that nigga Sharome. Best believe I'm trying my best to hold up my end of things, but since I ain't been able to make it happen just yet, I got two things for you. The first is this." He pulled out a desk drawer, reached in, and slapped two stacks of money on top of it. "This twenty racks right here. That should buy me some time because I appreciate you letting my girls loose and handling that bidness for my niggaz. This here is also somethin' else you gonna wanna see. And Kazi is, too, which is why I called the both of y'all here." He came out of the desk with a fistful of pictures and handed them to me to look over.

As soon as I looked down at them, my eyes got big as fuck. "When were these took?" I wanted to know.

"About two weeks ago. That's Sharome right there, and I guess he fucking wit' Ramsey and them Blood niggaz out in Harlem. The streets say he's his runner. That nigga over there clocking plenty paper. I know that nigga Ramsey personally, and he ain't no joke. He known for knocking niggaz's heads right off they shoulders. Been plugged with the Peru Bloodz ever since he was eight years old. Now he got it for the whole east coast. On top of that, his arm reaches all the way to California. He even got people in law enforcement that's way over yo' head in his pocket. He's a problem, fo' real."

I continued to look over the pictures as this fool told me shit I already knew. Me and Ramsey went way back. Back in the day he'd been an enemy of my Shotgun Posse. I think he was Rah'nell's cousin or something.

And then it all made sense. Rah'nell must've been the person Leesee ran to after she'd escaped the crib. I started to shake my head. I had a trick up my sleeve for that nigga.

Jelissa

Instead of handing the pictures to Kazi, I slammed them on the desk and picked up my twenty thousand dollars. "We even, nigga. Go on wit' yo' life. Don't worry about this shit no more. I got this." I bumped the shit out of Kazi on my way out the door.

An hour later I was having a hard time focusing in on the presentation in front of me. We'd just ushered ten girls through the backdoor of Simone's brothel and had them line up against the wall, where Simone was looking them over from head to toe. At that moment she was appraising a pretty Puerto Rican girl that couldn't have been more than fifteen years old. She made her turn in a circle while I sat on the couch and watched from a distance.

Savan came from the back of her house with a bottle of Cîroc, and three glasses. "I told you, Shotgun, that when I got this new batch of girls, you'd be the first one I got in contact with. They fresh off the presses. All of 'em virgins, and I'm giving them to you at a steal. Of course, I want to play around with a few of them for a couple of days." He laughed and set the glasses down on the table.

Simone went from one girl to the next, squeezing their booties and making them show her their breasts. Once they did, she felt them up and nodded her head, then either placed them to the left or right of her. All those to the right she was going to buy, and everyone she put to the left she was passing on. I'd watched this process take place on so many occasions.

When it was all said and done, she'd only chosen four of the girls.

Savan stood up with a frown on his yellow face. I didn't like this pretty-ass nigga. I don't know why, but he just rubbed me the wrong way. "Hey, what's the matter with these six over here?" he asked, looking her over closely.

Simone smiled. "I'll give you ten gees apiece for these four right here and right now. I ain't going no higher."

Savan turned to look at me. "Shotgun, what's good, man? You told me to order ten girls from Puerto Rico, and that's what I did. All virgins, man. I was expecting that hundred thousand we discussed. What gives?" He started to walk toward me.

I stood up and moved him out of the way aggressively. "Yo, Simone, you buyin' 'em all. That's that. I had to pull too many strings to get these li'l hoez up here. Now, a deal is a deal. Come off that bread, right now."

She shook her head. "I don't want all of them. I only want four. I ain't gon' know what to do with the rest of them. Besides, it's stupid to have all of the same hoez from one shipment living under your roof. Once they get comfortable, they always wind up plotting against you. Now, I'm taking the youngest four. That's these right here. The rest of these bitchez can go 'bout they bidness." She walked toward the back of the house, and I knew from experience she was going to get the forty gees for the girls. I watched her switch down the hallway and laughed.

Savan looked like he was about to lose his mind. "Damn, man, I thought everything was good. What happened, Shotgun?"

He stepped in front of me while the little girls huddled together and got to speaking in Spanish. I knew a little, and I was able to make out one of them saying the lady was going to split them up. Another asked what they were going to do. A third said they should tell her three of them were sisters. Another said she wouldn't care; they were all evil here.

I pushed Savan so hard he flew into their huddle and the girls separated, screaming as if they were in grave danger. While they were doing that, I knelt down and straddled this pretty-ass nigga and put my gun in his mouth. "Look here, nigga, don't you ever step yo' punk ass into my personal space again. If you do, I'll blow yo' head off. Let's get one thing perfectly clear: I don't like you. I don't gee for what you stand for, and I'm looking for a reason to body you. My acquaintance said she only want four of your girls, so that's all she gon' buy. Once she pays you, you take yo' money and the rest of these li'l hoez and get the fuck out of here, else it's gon' be trouble. Nod your head if you understand me?"

He did.

I got up just as Simone came back into the room and handed him his money. After the transaction was all said and done, I found myself parked in the parking lot of Leesee's old high school, missing her and formulating a plan in my mind to get my baby girl. The more I imagined her and Sharome together, the sicker it made me until I knew Rah'nell had to pay in the worst way.

I let my seat back and closed my eyes, sniffing Leesee's old panties I'd found in her laundry hamper.

Chapter 10

Leesee

I dropped the phone before the social worker could even finish what she was saying to me. All I'd heard was her saying they'd found the man I'd thought was my father for eighteen years stabbed to death in his cell at two in the morning. I fell to my knees and began vomiting all over the floor. I didn't know what to do. I wanted to call Sharome, but he'd already told me whenever he was on the road and handling bidness he would check in with me, and it wouldn't be smart for me to call him out the blue in case he was in the middle of a deal and the people he was dealing with thought he was confiding with the police. I didn't fully understand what that meant, but I just followed the rules. I couldn't stand for any problems.

So instead of calling him, I called Savan. I needed some type of kind words.

Two hours later I was sitting on his couch inside his living room with my head between my legs, feeling like life was more than a bitch. I honestly felt like I wanted to die. Even though I'd found out Rah'nell wasn't my real father, he'd always acted like one to me. I loved him with my whole heart and was devastated, to say the least.

Savan came into the room with a bottle of Cîroc and a box of Kleenex. He sat them on the table and knelt beside me. "Baby girl, is there anything I can do for you right now? Anything you need, just name it and I'll do it."

I blinked and tears ran down my cheeks. "Can you just hold me and tell me everything is going to be okay? I just need to be within your arms right now, Savan, please."

"Oh baby, sure thing," he said, climbing on the couch and wrapping me in his warm embrace.

Jelissa

As soon as I felt his big arms wrapped around me, I began to cry my little heart out. He rocked me back and forth and rubbed my back, giving me light kisses on my cheek and brushing my hair out of my face. "You're my little baby, Leesee, and it's okay, li'l mama. I'll be the best daddy I can for you from here on out. I promise. Just tell me what you need, and Daddy'll take care of it."

I cried harder as he held me tighter. I felt so safe and secure in his arms, but at the same time I felt weak and vulnerable because the only father I had ever known was gone. I truly wondered if Savan could step up to the plate. I already felt some type of way about him. "I just need you to be there for me, Savan. I need you to care for me and be my daddy. Protect me from this cold world, because nobody can protect a girl like a father can. I miss him so much," I whimpered.

He rocked back and forth with me and kissed me on the forehead. "I got you, baby. I'ma do all it takes. You'll see. In fact, Daddy knows just what you need right now." In one quick movement he picked me up and carried me up the stairs to his bedroom, laying me down slowly on the bed before getting on top of me. "I think you just need me to heal you right now, baby girl, is that it?" He leaned down and kissed both of my cheeks Before wiping my tears away.

I sniffed snot back into my nose and took a deep breath, trying to calm my emotions that were out of whack. I needed Savan to take me away. I needed to release my emotions into him. I nodded my head. "Yeah, I need you, Savan. Nobody is here for me right now. Only you are. Please heal me. Take me away from this pain."

In answer to that he pulled his tight wife beater over his head, exposing his muscular body that was all man. I closed my eyes as I felt him bite into my neck and take the handcuffs off his night stand, fastening them to my wrists. "Leesee, when I'm done with you this time, the only daddy you gon' need is me right here. I got you, boo." With that said, he ripped my blouse down the middle.

***

Rome

Ramsey threw his arm around my neck and lay his forehead against my own. We were at his estate on Staten Island, standing in his den, and in front of us was a table full of money, already in stacks of ten thousand. He kissed me on the cheek. "One month, Sharome. One fucking month, and you see what good hustling do?" he hollered and kissed my cheek again.

I smiled and shook my head. "How much is it?" My eyes were wide. It was a long table; the kind rich people ate at when they invited their whole family over for Thanksgiving dinner. Ramsey had already told me it was separated into piles of ten thousand, so I was guessing the number had to be all the way up there.

He let me go and jogged around the table as his three-armed bodyguards stood watch from the door. "This four million is in dirty money. Four muthafucking million dollars, and it's all because of you. All because of my li'l nigga hitting that highway and keeping shit one hunnit. So, you know what I'ma do? I'ma tell you what I'ma do. Two hunnit and fifty thousand of this is yours. And it's a gift. You don't owe me shit but to keep on doing like you been doing. Oh, that li'l bitch you got driving for you. This twenty gees is for her. Send her my regards and take her out somewhere nice tonight. She been one hunnit so far, so we gotta honor that in green. Yeah!" He clapping his hands together, scaring the shit out of me.

When I got home, there was nobody there but Tia. As soon as she saw me, she smiled, walked over, and wrapped her arms around my waist. "I'm so glad you're home. I was worried somethin' happened to you. What you been out there doing all night?" she asked, looking up at me.

I laughed and unleashed her arms from around me. "That fool Ramsey wanted to run some things by me. You already know how he is when he starts talking. Where is Leesee?" I made my way to our bedroom. I figured she was probably sleeping or something. On most days she preferred to lay in until I came home and woke her up.

Tia followed close behind me. "I don't know. She wasn't in when I came down this morning. After you dropped me off last night, I went straight upstairs. And this morning when I came down, I knocked on the door and she didn't answer me. Her whip ain't outside, either."

Before I could grab the knob and open our bedroom door, Tia grabbed my hand and stopped me, walking up to me and kissing me on the lips with her eyes closed. I allowed that to happen, then placed a hand on each of her shoulders and moved her backward. "Yo, we good, but chill, ma," I said softly as if Leesee was on the other side of the door. I didn't know what I was going to do about our situation just yet, though it was on my heart to tell Leesee everything that had taken place. I just felt so dirty, like I needed to come clean and let her know what was good.

Tia nodded her head before lowering it and walking the opposite way down the hall. I sensed she was worried, and I wanted to assure her she would be okay, but in that moment, I didn't know what I was going to do.

When I pushed in the door and found the bedroom empty, my heart dropped. I looked all around the room and even the bathroom, yet there was no trace of her. I felt sick to my stomach, like the world was closing in on me. I got to thinking the worst right off the back. I thought about Shotgun doing something to her, or Kazi. I thought about car accidents, rapists, kidnappers, and all kinds of other things that were slowly driving me crazy.

Love Me Even When It Hurts 2

I sat on the edge of the bed and began texting her phone, telling her to hit me back right away, that I missed her, and I loved her. To just tell me something. After sending those texts, I sat there with my head down, not knowing what to do. The room felt so cold without her there. I needed to know she was okay, that karma was not taking her away from me because of what me and Tia had done. My throat got tight, and I had to get up and pace the floor or I was going to lose my mind.

Tia stepped into the doorway about ten minutes later after I'd sent Leesee three more texts with no response. "Sharome, you gotta calm down. She's okay. I just got off of the phone with Shante, and she said Leesee's father, Rah'nell, was killed yesterday in the prison."

I stopped mid-pace. "Did she say where Leesee was? Like, has she gotten into contact with her? Or is she over there?" I asked, praying one of the things were true.

Tia shook her head. "Nall, she said she been trying to reach out to her, too, and she ain't responding to nobody. I don't know what's going on but worrying ain't gon' do nothin' but make things worse. Maybe she's out clearing her head, and when she gets her mind in order, she'll get back to you. In the meantime, is there anything I can do for you? Like, can I make you breakfast? Are you hungry?" she asked, walking up to me again and looking into my eyes with concern.

I shook my head. "Nah, not 'til I know what's good wit' her. But I could use a glass of orange juice, though. I'd appreciate that from you. Oh, and I got somethin' for you, too." I shook my head and made my way outside to my truck, opened the back door, and grabbed the duffle bag with the $270 thousand in it. The sun shined bright in the sky causing me to squint my eyes. There was a light breeze flowing throughout the city that felt real good to me. I felt like I needed a walk or something and would consider it after I finished giving Tia her piece of the money.

Jelissa

When I got back into the house, she was just finishing pouring the glass of orange juice. She handed it to me after I sat the bag on the floor, knelt down, and unzipped it. Taking a sip of the juice and placing the glass back on the table, I rifled through the duffle until I pulled out two ten thousand-dollar bundles and handed them to her. "Huh, this for you being so one hunnit. That fool Ramsey sends his love and regards, too."

She took the money with her eyes opened as wide as they could go. "Oh my god, how much is this?" She thumbed through it and bit into her bottom lip nervously.

I stood up, holding the bag by its strap, ready to take it into the room and place the contents in the safe. "That's twenty gees right there. That ain't got nothing to do with yo' weekly three. That's a bonus for you being so one hunnit. I know rolling wit' me ain't easy, but I appreciate you for standing on yo' gangsta. Word is bond, long as I'm eating, I'm gon' make sure you are, too. But thank you." I opened my arms and she stepped into them, hugging me with her eyes closed and a smile on her face.

Suddenly I heard footsteps on the porch, and then a key sliding into the lock. We broke our embrace and Tia stepped into the kitchen and opened the refrigerator, sticking her head inside it as if she was looking for something. A few seconds later the door opened inward and Leesee appeared with dark Ray Ban shades on her face.

I dropped the bag, ran over, and pulled her into my embrace, causing her glasses to fall off of her nose. She yelped loudly. I wrapped my arms around her. "Baby, baby, baby. I was so worried about you! Why didn't you answer my texts?" I asked, now feeling a little angry.

I took a step back and looked her over closely. She looked drowsy. There were bags under her eyes, and her hair was askew. She had her coat pulled all the way up to her chin, and she kept on fidgeting from side-to-side, avoiding eye contact with me.

Love Me Even When It Hurts 2

"I was gon' hit you back, but I was driving. I figured since I was on my way home anyway, I'd just talk to you when I got here. I'm sorry, baby. Please don't be mad at me. My dad died." She tightened her collar around her neck and, for the first time, looked up at me. Her eyes were watery, she blinked, and tears fell down her cheeks before she stepped closer and lay her head on my chest.

I pulled her into my embrace and placed my chin on the top of her head. For some reason I just didn't feel right. I felt like I was missing something. On top of that she smelled a little pungent. I held her for a few moments with my thoughts racing in my head. I looked over and saw Tia looking at us from the kitchen. Her lips were pursed, and she shook her head from side-to-side. We made eye contact before I looked off.

"I'm tired, baby. I just want to get in the shower, and then the bed. I feel like I can sleep for two days straight." She ended our embrace and made her way toward the bedroom, taking off her coat along the way.

After she disappeared down the hallway, Tia walked over to me and looked me up and down. "Sharome, you stupid. If you can't see what I see, then somethin' wrong." She poked me in the chest with her forefinger to emphasize her point.

I squinted my eyes at her, then looked down the hallway and saw Leesee close the bedroom door. "Baby, I'll be about twenty minutes. Don't disturb me, okay?" she yelled.

Now, hearing her say that made me a li'l irritated because she had never prevented me from interrupting her while she showered. Something didn't feel right. I wanted to go into our bedroom and check that shit out, but at the same time I wanted to hear what Tia had to say. "Yeah, a'ight, ma. I hear you!"

Tia slammed her money on the table and looked over at me, shaking her head in disgust. "You too soft with her, and you so dumb you can't even see she cheatin' on yo' ass. You can't see that?" she asked with ripples forming on her forehead.

Jelissa

Hearing that damn near took all of the breath out of my lungs. I felt a li'l dizzy. All of the sudden the crib felt like the thermostat on the heater was turned all the way up. My heart pounded in my chest, and I felt as sick as I did when I didn't know where Leesee was. I sat the bag on the floor and snatched Tia's ass up in anger. "What the fuck make you say that, Tia, huh? Didn't you just hear what she said? She was grieving over her old man. That's what the matter is. You'da been sick, too." I was having all of these visions in my head of multiple men laying Leesee down, and with each image I felt weaker and weaker.

Tia broke out of my embrace and fixed her blouse, looking up at me with anger. "You sittin' here snatchin' me up when you should be snatchin' her li'l ass up. That's what she need." She sucked her teeth loudly. "And I get the whole father thing, but didn't nobody know where she was, then she wearing the same fit I saw her in two days ago. Plus, she got that walk o' shame look written all over her face. Some nigga done sent her ass packing and didn't even let her get herself together first." She shrugged her shoulders. "But then again, what do I know?" She grabbed her money and made her way up the stairs, shaking her head, looking back at me one time before she disappeared out of my sight.

I sat down at the table for a moment to gather myself, head lowered, mind racing, feeling like I was about to either pass out or snap the fuck out. I jumped up, snatched the bag up from the floor, and made my way to the bedroom, twisting the knob and finding it locked. That pissed me all the way off.

Now I knew something wasn't right. I got to beating on it loudly and was seconds away from kicking that muthafucka in.

Chapter 11

Leesee

Doom! Doom! Doom! "Open this muthafuckin' door, Leesee! Why is it locked, anyway?" Sharome yelled, and I could tell he was angry.

I stepped out of the shower, wrapped a towel around my body, and put another one around my hair, making sure it hung carelessly so it could cover up the suck marks Savan had left all around my neck. My wrists were raw from the handcuffs. My ass cheeks felt tender, and my kitty was on fire. Savan had freaked me the whole night through, doing things to me I couldn't believe I'd let him do, and now I was paying for it.

"Here I come, Sharome. Baby, just calm down," I said, looking around at the door as it rattled from his loud pounding. I opened it and he stormed inside, nearly knocking me over. "Damn, what's the matter?" I asked, already knowing what was good.

He dropped a duffle bag on the floor and turned around with a scowl on his face. One I had never seen before. "Where the fuck you coming from, Leesee, huh? And don't feed me no bullshit, because I'm seconds away from snapping, on some real shit."

I felt my stomach drop. "Baby, I told you. Rah'nell got killed, so I needed some air. That's all. Why are you charging me up like this?" I felt ready to panic. For as long as Sharome and I had been together, he'd never come at me in a hostile manner the way he was that day. I felt like he suspected something, as if the fact I had slept with Savan was written all over my face.

Sharome shook his head. "Nall, I ain't going for that shit. I get that yo' old man passed and all, and I'ma support you as best I can after I get some answers, but you gon' give me them first. I need to know where you laid your head. Keep that shit one hunnit, too."

He flared his nostrils, then rolled his head around on his neck. I knew from experience he only did that when he was trying to calm down. I felt he was on the verge of spazzing out, and I didn't know what that would mean for me. After all, he was Shotgun's son. It was in his DNA to lose his wig in anger.

I felt as small as an ant. The walls felt as if they were closing in on me. Sweat appeared on my neck, and I couldn't stop myself from shaking. I was scared out of my mind, worried I would be found out. I couldn't stand to lose Sharome. I couldn't stand to be without him, especially after I'd lost Rah'nell. Sharome was the only one left on Earth who I knew without a shadow of a doubt loved me with all of his heart.

I lowered my head and swallowed. "I. I. I slept in my car. I just didn't feel like being bothered, so I rolled around New York until I got tired, then I parked in the lot of CVS over on 139th and passed out. I didn't wake up until your texts came through this morning," I lied. I didn't know what else to say. There was no way I was going to tell him about Savan. Not like that. He'd leave me for sure.

Sharome looked me over for a long time without uttering a word. Just looked me up and down, then shook his head. "You think I'm a muthafuckin' fool, Leesee. I mean, I'm crazy about you and everything, and I love you more than anybody on this earth, but ain't nothin' stupid about me."

He continued to mug me, then walked into his closet, knelt down, and moved his shoeboxes out of the way, followed by the loose piece of wall before pulling out his safe and opening it. Then he grabbed the duffle bag, unzipped it, and took out bundle after bundle of money, placing it in his safe. He stopped, turned around, and tossed a knot up to me. "That's ten gees. You gotta start saving yo' money. You might need to get you a safe or somethin'." He emptied the entire bag into the safe, then closed it and put it back into the wall, tossing the bag in the closet and closing the door.

I stood there like a damn fool, not knowing what to do or say. I felt his last comment was a direct shot at me, like he was trying to tell me in so many words that I needed to start saving up my money because he was going to leave me soon. I felt my knees get weak, and then the tears came. "Sharome, are you thinking about leaving me?" I whimpered. "Please tell me the truth."

He turned his back on me and went into the bathroom, running the water, taking a bar of soap, and thoroughly washing his hands. "Yo, I don't know what I'ma do yet. My brain screwed up. You lying to me and shit is throwing me off. I don't even know you no more." He blew air through his teeth loudly and shook his head, then walked past me and opened his closet, taking out a black-and-white Marc Jacobs fit. He reached up onto his top shelf, grabbing a black-and-white Yankees cap, then down for a box of Airmax 90s. He tossed them all onto the bed and took his shirt and vest off, going around the room as if I wasn't even standing there. Every time he walked past me, ignoring my presence, I wanted to die more and more.

I jumped into his path as he attempted to walk back into the bathroom. "Sharome, please. I swear I didn't do nothin' wrong, baby. I fell asleep in my car. I was depressed and you told me to not reach out to you when you were out busting moves, so I didn't know what to do. Do you have any idea how bad I felt that I couldn't even reach out to my man after I found out my father had been killed in prison?" I fell to my knees for dramatic effect. "I needed you so bad and you weren't even there to hold me. You left me all alone, and I was angry, baby. Angry, so I didn't answer my phone, but I swear I was in my car the whole time. I haven't done anything wrong. I love you so much. Please don't leave me, because I need you," I cried with all of my might, holding him around the waist and placing my cheek against his hip. I imagined him leaving me, and I knew I wasn't strong enough to take it. I felt bad about lying to him, but in that moment, I was in a fight for my life. I needed him so, so badly. He was all I had.

Sharome dropped down to his knees immediately and wrapped his arms around me, holding me tight. He kissed me on the forehead. "Baby, calm down. It's gon' be okay, damn. You already know I will never leave your side. I love you way too fucking much. I just don't like when you get to acting out of character. I didn't know what was good, then we got all these enemies that's gunning for us, so what was I supposed to think other than the worst?"

He rubbed my back, then lifted my chin so I could look into his eyes. The scent of his cologne wafted up my nose. I shook my head. "I'm so sorry, baby. I swear I will never do that again. It wasn't fair, and I promise I'm going to be better. Just please don't leave me. I need you."

He nodded his head, then kissed my lips, brushing my hair out of my face and wiping my tears away. "On everything I stand for, I will never leave you, Leesee. You are my everything, and neither one of us is perfect. Now, far as your story go, if you're saying that is what happened, then I'm forced to believe you. The only thing that's throwing me off is all of these passion marks around your neck."

As soon as he said that, I looked down and noted the towel I'd had around my head was now on the floor. My stomach dropped as if I was on a roller coaster. I watched him stand up and shake his head, laughing to himself. He grabbed his outfit and made his way into the bathroom. "Yo, it's good, ma. I don't wanna know what happened. Let's just move on from this day and promise to be better."

That evening happened an entire week ago, and things between me and him had been tense ever since. I didn't know if deep down in his heart of hearts he was planning on leaving me or if he was actually, seriously willing to put things behind us, but I found it odd he didn't even ask for an explanation. So, a week after we'd had our little run-in I waited until he came home and pulled him into our bedroom, sitting him down so I could let him know where I stood. At the time I wasn't sure how much I was going to tell him, but my nerves were getting the better of me, and I needed to feel him out. After he sat down, I took a deep breath, walked over and closed our bedroom door, and stood before him.

***

Rome

"Baby, I just gotta be perfectly honest with you because I wasn't a week ago, and I feel like you deserve the absolute truth."

It felt like it was a million degrees in the room. I prepared myself to hear the worst news I knew she was about to tell me, though I'd already mentally had the conversation in my mind over a hundred times before today. I rolled my head around on my neck and exhaled slowly. "G'on 'head. All I ask is you don't leave nothin' out. Tell me everything or don't tell me nothin' at all, because like I told you, I'm already past this in my head," I lied. I think for me not knowing felt better than knowing the truth. I don't know why that was, but it was just how I felt deep down.

Leesee stood before me and sighed. She rubbed her hands over her pretty face and shook her arms out. "Okay, okay. But, baby, just hear me out. Can you do that?"

I nodded. "Yeah, just spit it out and let's get this over wit'." I felt myself becoming a little irritated because it felt like we were picking at an old wound. Plus, I didn't know if I had the gall to tell her about me and Tia. I preferred to keep all that swept under the rug. I just wanted to move forward.

She nodded her head. "Okay. Well, here goes nothin'." She faced me but didn't look me in the eye. "Sharome, I lied to you. I was with somebody a week ago, and I'm not proud of it. I stayed with him the whole night after I found out Rah'nell had been killed. I really wanted to call you so I could receive your support, but I remembered you said to never call you when you were away on business. Knowing all of that, and feeling how I was feeling, I grew vulnerable and made a mistake of spending a night with another man, solely for his support," she said, finally looking me in the eyes.

I felt myself becoming heated because I imagined another dude on top of her, sucking all over her neck while she moaned and called out his name. I didn't have it in me to imagine them fucking. I would have lost my mind. "So, what, you let him smash, too?" I asked, harsher than I actually meant to.

Leesee lowered her head and avoided my eyes again. "Hell nall, I would never do that. But there was some heavy petting. Like, he gave me those hickies, and he tried to take things a little further, but I stopped him. Once he saw I wouldn't let him get what he was shooting for, he put me out, and I spent the rest of the night in my car, feeling guilty about all I'd done with him. I know it wasn't right, baby, and I'm so, so sorry. You have to believe me. I was vulnerable and angry because I needed you to be there for me, but I couldn't even call you for support. I felt horrible." She covered her face with her hands, sobbing.

Now I felt sick because she'd had enough love for me to tell me what actually happened that night, and there I was with my own secrets, but I didn't have the balls to let her know what was good between me and Tia. "What's his name, Leesee?" I needed to know if I knew him. I prayed it wasn't one of the homies from the hood. I'd only brought a few of them around her before, so I didn't know. But had it been one of them, I was sure I was going to kill his ass. There was no doubt about that.

"Savan. I met him at school. He's older, and it just happened, baby. Please know I am dying here. I never meant to hurt you. You're my everything." She walked to me and knelt down between my legs, looking up at me. "Can we get through this?"

I was doing everything I could to clear my brain from seeing images of her and some older dude, but a part of me was thankful I didn't know him. If I had, I knew for a fact I would have bodied him that night. "Just kill that shit, Leesee, and let's move on. Let's make today our first day and put whatever sins we got between each other to rest. You cool wit' that?"

She nodded. "Long as you still love me the same way, then yeah, I'm cool with that."

We stood up, and I held her face while I looked into her eyes. "Are you sure I can trust you the way I thought I was able to? You sure you don't need more than me?" I rubbed her cheeks with my thumbs.

She sucked her bottom lip and sniffled. "You can trust me, baby. I won't mess up no more. I promise, baby."

Later that night me and Tia hopped on the road on our way up to Albany, where we'd meet up with the Arian's white boys so they could give me a new shipment of meth. I was told by Ramsey that I would be picking up four suitcases' worth, which made me a little nervous because prior to that day I'd never picked up more than two suitcases full.

On the way there I couldn't get the conversation I'd had with Leesee off of my brain. There were so many questions I wanted to ask her that I hadn't because I was sure I wasn't strong enough to handle their truths. Questions like how long she and Savan had been creeping around. What was the furthest they'd ever went? Was he the one who had gotten her into the whole choking thing? Did she start to screw around with him because she felt I didn't meet her sexual needs, like Tia had said she eventually would? I loved her so much that I didn't know what to do. I was stuck and sick at the same time.

Tia must've picked up on my mood because she reached and turned the system down, then grabbed my hand just as I was pulling onto the highway. "Sharome, you can talk to me about anything. Whatever is going on in your brain, you don't have to handle it all alone. What's good?"

I switched over two lanes of traffic and stepped on the gas, passing a brown station wagon that had big clouds of black smoke coming from its exhaust. I let down my sun visor. The sun was just starting to set, and the red glare it cast made it hard for me to see in front of me until I lowered the visor. "Yo, grab that blunt out the ashtray and put some fire to it. I need to ease me mind, then I'll let you know what's good." I pulled down the ashtray and handed the weed-filled cigar to her.

She lowered her window just a crack, took her lighter, and lit the tip, inhaling and blowing the smoke back out. "She was cheating on you, huh?"

I nodded. "Yeah, wit' some older nigga. She said she ain't fuck him or nothin', but I don't know if I believe that, especially after seeing all them passion marks on her neck. But I didn't check her, either. A part of me didn't want to know. I mean, we just as guilty."

She handed me the blunt and I took three quick pulls off of it and inhaled deeply. I was praying I felt the effects right away. I needed to escape the mental pains I was going through. No matter how much I made it seem like it wasn't a big deal to me, inside I was torn up over the fact I wasn't enough for her, that she needed another man to fill in the blanks. An older man, at that. Damn, my self worth was shattered. I was on the brink of breaking down.

Tia took the blunt from me and pulled on it, sitting back in her seat. "I would've never came at you if I didn't think she wasn't doing her own thing on the side. I'd heard her on the phone more than once talking all lovey-dovey to some dude, and I knew it couldn't have been you because on more than one occasion you were in the back room and she was in the kitchen."

I raised my right eyebrow and gave her a crazy look. "And where were you?"

Love Me Even When It Hurts 2

"At the top of the stairs, on my way down, but you should already know I'm nosey, so I stood right where I could hear her and just listened. My cousin somethin' else. She don't know how good of a man you are. She really don't know what she has. You see, she got them daddy issues real tough because Shotgun been going in on her ever since she was little, so that's all she know. That's why as soon as she got away from his ass, she still had to find her an older man. She's replacing him with somebody just like him. It's crazy, but I understand. It is what it is. I don't feel guilty about what we've done thus far, and I ain't about to let us stop, either. I'm trying to keep my feelings out of all of this, but if I'm being honest, that's the hardest thing in the world for me. I care about you already, and I know for a fact I would never choose any man over you. I see what you are, and I would never make that mistake. Shid, I'm cool wit' just being yo' side piece until you want to take things further." She reached over and squeezed my thigh like she always seemed to do when we were driving. "Sharome, she ain't gon' stop fuckin' wit' the dude, trust me. If it ain't him, then it's gon' be some other older nigga, because it's in her to yearn for them types. It ain't nothin' against you because she can't help it."

I shook my head and looked over at her. "So, what you sayin'? Is this somethin' I gotta accept because it's the way it's always goin' to be or somethin'?" I didn't know if I could ever be cool with that. I mean I loved Leesee and all, but I loved her because I thought she needed me, that I was her one and only. I was too jealous to allow her to fuck wit' some other nigga on the side, then come and crawl in the bed wit' me after knowing where she'd been all night. I was pretty sure that was a deal breaker for me, though I couldn't imagine life without her by my side. She was the first person with whom I'd ever felt real love. I needed her, and I felt I just needed to figure this whole thing out. Maybe we could go to some kind of counseling or something. I would be down for that. I loved her that much.

Tia shrugged her shoulders. "I'm saying that might be the case, so why fight it? You ain't gotta leave her. I would never advise that. I say we just keep on doing our own thing, and you support her as much as you can. And when things get too rough for you, then just come to me. I'll be your crying shoulder. I'll never turn you away. You got my word on that." She squeezed my thigh again, then leaned over and sucked my ear lobe into her mouth. "Mm, you gon' always taste good to me and fill me up. My word is bond on that." She sat back in her seat with a smile on her face.

I tried my best to focus on the task at hand, though everything she was saying was taking a toll on me. I didn't want to lose Leesee, and I didn't want things to change so much around us that we lost that love we had for each other. In my mind there wasn't a woman on Earth that made me feel how she made me feel. I always felt she was my one true love, and I wasn't willing to change my feelings on that. As far as Tia went, she was definitely a nice slice of forbidden fruit. She said all the right things, made all the right moves, and always seemed to be there when I was at my lowest points. I didn't know how I truly felt about her. One thing I did know was she was no Leesee. No one was. I didn't crave any other woman but her, and we needed to figure things out so we could get through it. I felt like I would fight and face any battle with her.

"Ain't you gon' say somethin', Sharome?" Tia asked, turning all the way in her seat so she was facing me.

"All I'ma say right now, Tia, is stay in yo' lane. Just keep on doing what you're doing, and if you see me falling, be there to pick me up. I know I'ma need you one day. A'ight?"

She sucked her bottom lip into her mouth loudly. "Yeah, a'ight. I'ma do just that."

Chapter 12

Rome

The rain spattered into my face just as the wind picked up and made it hard for me to stand still without feeling like I was about to topple over. My sock felt wet in my right Airmax shoe after stepping in a puddle of water. I looked back at my truck as lighting flashed through the sky and was followed up by the roaring of thunder. I pulled my Marc Jacobs hood over my head as I walked to the barn door and beat on it with all of my might.

I waited for a full minute and was about to turn away when I heard sounds on the other side of the red barn door. I hated the fact I went through this same procedure every single time.

The big door swung inward. The light from the inside lit up my face and the dark night behind me. In front of me stood a big, fat, bald white man who had to be every bit of six feet, eight inches tall and four hundred pounds. A big swastika was tatted on his bald head.

He looked down at me while chewing on a piece of hay. "Hey there, little buddy. I see you's right on time. Come on in." He stepped to the side so I could pass him.

The first thing I noted was the rank odor of ass and sweat coming off his body. On top of that, he smelled like a wet canine. I stepped into the barn and looked around. There were about six other dudes inside, and all of their eyes were on me. I was feeling real uneasy, especially when he closed the big barn door. I started to worry about Tia almost immediately. I wondered if she was scared out there in the rain all by herself. I needed to get back to her.

"Yo, what's good? Ramsey say I'm supposed to pick up four suitcases. Y'all got them ready yet, or what?" I asked, looking up at the giant.

Jelissa

He broke into a fit of laughter, holding his big belly that poked way out of his overalls. He looked over his shoulder back at his men, and they joined in the laugh.

I didn't understand what was so funny. I scrunched my face, ready to go into the small of my back and pull my .45 out and get to busting. Something wasn't right. I felt it deep within my soul. "Say, what's so funny, big boy?"

His face went from that of happiness to that of anger. "Well, it's been brought to my attention that your boss has been low-balling us white boys, and I for one don't like it." He spit the hay on the ground and took a step toward me.

Thunder boomed overhead, and as I looked over his shoulder, I saw two of his men loading shotguns. I bucked my eyes and got ready to grab my heater. "Yo, I'm just the delivery boy. I don't know what y'all really got going on. He tells me what to drop off and pick up, that's it," I said, taking a step back. I could smell the rain and the wet grass outside. I started to panic because I knew Tia and I were out in the middle of nowhere. Those white dudes could have killed us and buried us in a cornfield. Ramsey was supposed to have a security team following us around, but after the second week he'd called them off. I guess he figured he could trust me. Now I was wishing he had been more careful.

"Well, all you do is represent a piece of his operation to us, which means if we make an example out of his pesky delivery boy, then he knows we're not the ones to be fucked with. I already don't like you filthy niggers. Should've known to not go into business with ya."

He stepped forward, and I thought he was about to try and grab me. I upped that .45 and slammed it right under his chin. "Say, man. Look, I don't know what the fuck you and Ramsey got going on, but that shit ain't got nothin' to do wit' me. Now, I'll pass him any message you want, but you finna let me up out of here. That's how this gon' work." I wrapped my arm around his neck and pulled his big ass down into a headlock almost.

116

Love Me Even When It Hurts 2

"You stupid son of a bitch. How far you think you're gonna make it if you pull that trigger? Huh?"

I started to walk backward toward the door as thunder boomed somewhere off in the distance. His men surrounded me with their guns raised. "Look, I don't wanna pull this trigger. I ain't got shit against you or them, but y'all ain't finna do me like this. Take that shit up with Ramsey." I continued to walk backward. "Tell yo' boys to back off. Now! Word is bond, you gon' die before I do. We can meet that reaper tonight, together." I jammed the gun even harder under his chin.

"Alright, you son of a bitch. Just get the fuck out of here and tell Ramsey to go fuck himself, that we're dealing with the chinks now, and they are way better businessmen. Tell that monkey to go peel a banana," he spat.

Though he was talking all that tough shit, he kept right on allowing me to pull his ass in the direction of the door. "Tell one of them to open the door. Hurry up!" I tightened my headlock just enough to let him know I was serious. "Tell 'em, you racist bitch!"

"Chucky, open the damn door and let this nigger out. He won't get away with this, you can bet your bippy on that."

I ain't know what the word bippy meant, but one thing I did know was I wasn't letting his ass go until me and Tia were in the clear. I knew them white boys would've had no problem killing us out there and disposing of our bodies. They were already dealing with a lot of chemicals because of the meth they cooked all day long, so I wasn't going. I had to get us the fuck up out of there, and fast.

As soon as Chucky swung open the door, the rain blew in from outside, drenching me fast. The wind picked up and made a low-pitch howl as it whistled through the night. The constant sound of rain hitting pavement was loud in my ears. I continued to walk with this big oaf in a headlock, dragging his ass toward my truck.

Jelissa

As I got outside with the rain attacking me, Tia must've saw what was taking place because the next thing I knew my headlights came on and she stuck her head out of the passenger's window. "Sharome, what's good?" she hollered with water dripping off her face.

I pointed to the driver's side. "Yo, start the whip, ma. These racist muthafuckas on bullshit. We gotta get up out of here."

The big oaf's army ran outside with their shotguns raised. Chucky stepped to the side of us with a scowl on his wet face. "Randy, I ain't letting this nigger take you no damn where. He's gonna have to kill all of us. Ain't that right, boys?"

Chick-chick! Chick-chick! The sounds of their guns being cocked all around me sounded through the rain. I started to panic. Leesee's face crossed my mind. I wasn't trying to go out like this. I had to see her one more time. I had to tell her I loved her, and we could get through absolutely anything. That she was my life.

I tightened my hold on Randy's neck. "Randy, tell yo' men to stand down. Now, I'm just the delivery man. Y'all ain't gon' accomplish shit by hurting me. Trust me, you ain't doing nothin' but waging war wit' Ramsey." I continued to pull him toward my truck as lightning flashed across the sky and the wind seemed to pick up, making it hard to keep my balance.

Chucky upped his shotgun and put it to the side of my cheek. "Tell me what to do, Randy, or I'm gon' make my own decision and kill this monkey!" he screamed as if he was losing his mind.

I swallowed as I felt my stomach drop. Chucky pressed his barrel harder into my cheek, and his army of goons surrounded me.

***

Leesee

I stormed into Savan's apartment with my head down. My head felt as if it was spinning like a top. He stepped to the side, and I noticed he was holding a bottle of Moët. The heat from his penthouse warmed me almost immediately and made me feel uncomfortable. I took ten paces past the front door and turned around to face him.

"Look, Savan, I can't stay long. I just came to tell you it's over between us. I told my boyfriend everything, and he's willing to forgive me. So, it's been fun. Thank you for being there for me when I needed you, but this should be the last time we speak to or see each other again. Okay?" I said, damn near out of breath.

Savan closed the door to his place and gave me a little smile as if he was confused. He locked the door, then slowly walked over to me after setting the bottle of champagne on the table beside his loveseat. Then he walked over to me and held his arms open. "Baby, come here and tell Daddy what you're talking about. I'm not clearly understanding you."

I felt chills go down my spine at hearing him utter the word 'daddy.' I didn't know why that word was such a weakness of mine, but it literally made me melt. I felt his big arms wrap around me, and I don't know why I didn't stop him from completing the hug, but the next thing I knew he was holding me and kissing my neck softly. "Talk to me, baby. Tell daddy what the problem is."

I felt my knees go weak. Had he not been holding me up, I would have surely sunk to the ground. The scent of his cologne sailed up my nose, further intoxicating me and sending me on a mental journey that, in that moment, I didn't want to travel. Scenes from our past passion-filled nights replayed themselves in my mind as I closed my eyes and felt him hold me as only a man could. I found myself shaking and afraid.

Jelissa

"Look, Savan, we can't do this anymore. I love my man, and I have to respect him as well as myself. I have to let you go, but I thank you for all you've done. Please understand."

He rubbed up my back until his fingers were walking all over my scalp, and then he grabbed a handful of my hair and yanked my head backward, exposing my neck. I yelped in pain before I felt his teeth bite into my neck as if he was a vampire. He walked me backward and crashed me into the front door, licking my neck, then pressing his lips against my left ear. "It sounds to me like you trying to leave yo' daddy, but I ain't gon' let that happen. Not now, not ever. You get my drift?" He tightened his grip in my curls and yanked on my hair roughly.

"Ah! Please, Savan. We can't do this anymore. Just let me go. I should've never come here today," I cried, extending my hands to push him away from me.

He laughed, then shook his head. "Nah, I ain't going for that. I know when a little girl needs her daddy, and right now you're calling out for me, so let's just do what we gotta do."

He picked me up and carried me upstairs to his bedroom once again, then tossed me on his bed, but this time I jumped up and made a run for the door before he jumped in my path with a mug on his face. "You ain't leaving me, Leesee. I own you, girl. You gave me all rights to you, and I ain't giving 'em back." He grabbed me and threw me to the floor, then ran and threw open the top drawer on his dresser, reaching inside and taking out a pair of handcuffs.

"No! No! No!" I struggled to get to my feet. I had to get to the door and out of his place. I couldn't let him have my body again. I'd promised Sharome it was all over. I should have never come to his penthouse, should've had more common sense than that.

As soon as I got to my feet, he tackled me to the floor and slapped one of the handcuffs around my wrist. He picked me up again and tossed me on the bed, taking the cuffs and looping them around the metal piece on the headboard before clicking it on my other wrist. Luckily the chain in between the cuffs was about ten inches long, so it gave me a little freedom. I kicked my legs out at him, trying to make contact. I didn't know if I was trying to hurt him or not. I think I just wanted to put up as much of a fight as possible before the inevitable happened.

He took two big, red pieces of satin out of the drawer, grabbed my left ankle, and tied it to bed post by the foot of the bed, then grabbed the right and did the same while I struggled against my bonds, wiggling one way and then the next in an attempt to free myself. "Let me go, Savan! I don't want to do this. Please don't make me," I whimpered.

He stood at the foot of the bed and slowly peeled his shirt off with a smile on his handsome face. Once the shirt had been shed, he took his wife beater and pulled it over his head, exposing the body that had been driving me absolutely nuts for the last few weeks. "I've been here before, Leesee, but you know just like I know that li'l boy you messing with ain't got nothin' on me, baby girl. He can't do the things Daddy do for you. That's why you really came home to me even after you promised him it was over between you and I. Admit it."

He crawled onto the bed and made his way along my body. I shook my head from side to side, the feeling of being bound once again by him doing things to my womanly places that I couldn't deny. I felt my juices leaking into my panties. I wanted so bad to squeeze my thighs together, but the way he had me spread apart made that impossible. "No, Savan. I came here like a woman. I needed to break up with you in person. I had to give you more respect than to try and end things over the phone as if I were an immature woman. Uh! Shit!" I moaned.

He'd pulled my skirt all the way up, along with the crotch of my panties, forcing my sex lips to appear on each side of the laced material. Then, with one sex lip at a time, he sucked them into his mouth while he rubbed the other one. "I'm Daddy, and you're my baby girl. He can't do you like I can.

Admit it." He pulled the crotch further into me and sucked at my damp panties, slurping my juices through the material.

I arched my back, as much as I tried not to, offering myself to his mouth. "Please don't do this, Savan. Let me up so I can go home."

He yanked my panties to the side, exposing my entire kitty. "I am your home, baby girl. With me is where your heart is." He covered my kitty with his entire mouth, then forced his tongue into my slit and up my hole. It stabbed back and forth more than fifty times before he sucked on my clitoris as if he were mad at me.

I could feel the beads of sweat on my forehead. My hips constantly humped off the bed and into his mouth. My eyes were closed, and I begged for relief. I needed it so, so bad. "Savan. Savan. Ooh, baby. Please, I am begging you to just…" I whimpered, biting into my bottom lip.

He spread my sex lips further apart and nipped at my clit with his teeth, then sucked on it as if it were a nipple. I felt two of his fingers slide into me, and then they were going at full speed. "Tell me I'm Daddy! Tell me you need me, Leesee!" Back to sucking and fingering.

The sex noises coming from his mouth were driving me insane. I could feel his goatee rubbing against my naked lips. I was humping up off the bed in a frenzy. The predicament I found myself in was shamefully arousing to me. Mix that with the fact this older man seemed to really know my body, and no matter how hard I tired to not respond to his administrations I couldn't help it, and it all was a recipe for disaster.

He slid his left hand up my body and under my bra, pulling my right nipple, and that's when I came as hard as I ever have before in my life, screaming at the top of my lungs. "Ah! Savan! Ooh! Ah!" As the waves washed over me, I humped upward again, again, and again while he kept right on sucking at my clitty.

Love Me Even When It Hurts 2

After my body stopped its sexual convulsions, he climbed up my body and grabbed my neck. I could feel his hard penis poking at my side. It throbbed along my rib cage, poking me with anger. He squeezed harshly on my neck, so tight I really couldn't breathe. My eyes got big as saucers, and I began to panic.

"Tell me you belong to me. Tell me who Daddy is," he growled before licking the side of my face and jockeying for position between my legs. I could feel him kicking off his pants and boxers before his dick head was up against my sex lips, already causing them to separate around his helmet. He released his grip just a tad so I could talk.

"You are my daddy, Savan. Oh my god, only you," I managed, out of breath. The feel of his helmet throbbing against me caused me to become wetter and wetter. I could feel my juices running out of me and down into my ass crack. The vulnerability of it all was driving me crazy.

He sucked on my neck and bit me. "Beg Daddy for this dick! Beg me to put it in you, baby girl. I know you need it! Daddy knows!" He slid both of his hands under my bra and massaged my titties, pulling on the nipples while his penis throbbed against my middle. He rubbed it up and down my slit without actually penetrating me. I felt tortured.

"Unh! Please fuck me, Daddy! Please. I need you to, so bad." I humped into him and wanted to cry when Sharome's face popped into my mind. I couldn't believe what I'd just said, and even more than that, how bad I actually meant it. I needed to feel him deep within my womb. Needed to feel him turn into the brute he was. Needed to feel him sex me like a savage.

He licked his thumbs and spread my pussy lips apart, then took his big dick that looked like a dark brown cucumber full of veins, bit into his lower lip, and frowned at me. "Watch me, baby girl. Please watch Daddy do this," he ordered.

I gasped, out of breath, and watched as he spread my lips wide, then slammed his dick into me with so much force I came, flopping up and down like a fish out of water. "Oh! Daddy!" One ripple hit me after the next, then I felt him pounding me with what seemed like all of his might.

Bam. Bam. Bam. "You belong." *Bam. Bam. Bam.* "To me." *Bam. Bam. Bam.* He placed his hands around my neck and choked me for what had to be about ten seconds, and then he released me and kept on plowing into my middle, driving me into the bed, stuffing me again and again.

I felt so embarrassed by how many times I came while he did his thing to me while I was handcuffed to the bed, but I really felt ashamed when he un-cuffed me forty minutes later, lay on his back, and made me ride him with my back to his face. He held my ass and continued to slam me down on his penis, and every so often he'd smack my cheeks, sending ripples throughout my body. He made me turn around, and I leaned down. We sucked all over each other's lips loudly. Our tongues wrestled while he felt all over me with my hips grinding forward, taking as much of his pipe into me as I could. Our scents were heavy in the air. Sweat dripped off of my body and landed on his, and we kept on going.

Every time he would remind me that he was my daddy, it would spark somethin' deep within me, and I'd find myself yearning for more and more of him. I tried my best to not think about Sharome because every time I did, I felt so guilty and knew I was betraying him again, but there was just a part of me he really could not fulfill. It had to be an older man. An older man who could dominate me and treat me the way I needed to be treated. But at the same time, I really did need Sharome's love. Sharome had a love for me I had never felt before. A love I craved.

So, I found myself stuck between a rock and a hard place as Savan grabbed my ass and made me fuck into him harder and faster. "Uh!" I threw my head back with my face toward the ceiling, shaking and cumming again.

It ended with Savan laying me on my stomach, opening my butt cheeks, and running his tongue up and down my crease, sucking on my anal ring loudly. "You belong to me, Leesee. You're my little lady. Never forget that. Me and you are forever, baby. We were meant to be." Then his tongue slid into me again.

"Unh!" I closed my eyes and moaned deep within my throat, arching my back to feel him better.

As I opened my eyes again, I nearly fell out of the bed as I saw her. The sight freaked me all the way out as she stood at the edge of the bed with her hands duct taped together, along with her mouth. I looked over my shoulder at him as he feasted on my charms with his eyes closed, making as much noise as he possibly could.

"Savan, who the hell is that?!" I hollered.

Jelissa

Chapter 13

Shotgun

I felt the cool air blow into my face from my car's air conditioner. It helped me calm down as I sank lower behind the steering wheel and watched Kazi lean his head into a blue Chevy Caprice classic, take the pistol the passenger handed him, and place it into the small of his back before looking both ways and shaking up with the occupant. Then he hit the roof of the car twice before it pulled off down the streets, blowing the horn once.

Rain continued to beat against my windshield. It sounded like someone was pouring a big bag if rice little by little on top of my roof. I watched Kazi jog on the side of the apartment complex with his hood pulled over his head. I waited for about two minutes before I got out of my car into the pouring rain, popping my hood over my head and slamming the door. As thunder growled in the sky, I made my way across the residential empty street and followed along the same path he had. It was time to put an end to all of the games. There was no way I could continue on in life without knowing Kazi was no longer breathing. I knew the man had a deep hatred for me, and the more he moved upward in the Crip organization, the more of a threat he became. It was too risky. He had to go.

As I got to the back of the building where the parking lot was located, I stopped and peeked around the corner. He was nowhere to be found, which meant he must've already gone inside of the building. I jogged over to the door, feeling my denim pants stick to me. Once there, I pulled the door open as it had been left cracked by the use of a wet newspaper. I pulled out my Glock .40 pistol and slowly made my way into the hallway with it held at eye level. I squared my shoulders and

Jelissa

crouched down just enough to feel secure, about the same height they had taught us in the academy.

The first thing I saw in the hallway was a stairwell that led upstairs. Behind it was a series of apartment doors. I knew if Kazi was there, which I knew he was, he'd taken the stairs to the highest level. That was the sixth floor, so I traveled up the flights if stairs until I got there. When I got to the top, I was completely taken off guard.

Chick-chick! Chick-chick! Chick-chick! I heard the sounds of multiple guns being cocked all around me. Right smack dab in the middle of all of the bangers who were heavily armed and aiming their guns at me was Kazi holding two .44 Desert Eagles with a mug on his face. I was about to turn around when two more bangers appeared at the bottom of my flight with their handguns raised up at me.

"Uh-unh, nigga. Yo' punk ass ain't going nowhere. We finna handle this shit once and for all. Drop that pistol, cuz," Kazi said, stepping forward with both guns turned sideways, his upper lip curled and face an angry scowl.

I shook my head. "Nah, fuck that. You niggaz gon' kill me, you gon' bury me wit' my gun." I upped it and aimed it at Kazi.

He lowered his eyes into slits, smiling down at me.

"Just in case you boys don't know, I'm a part of the Newark Police Department. I am the muthafuckin' police. I have backup on the way, and they should be here in no time. Now, if any of you li'l niggaz wanna make it out of this situation without the whole state of New Jersey putting its foot up yo' ass, I'd advise you to walk away and leave this between me and this perpetrator, right here. This is your last warning." I yelled, looking behind me and then back up to Kazi, who had a sly grin on his face. I noted that none of his men moved a muscle.

"Fuck you and them other pork muthafuckas." He looked to the side and spit out a loogie. "Shotgun, on some real shit, you always been a bitch-ass nigga. We can take shit to the roof

128

and knuckle up, cuz. Fight until it's one of us standing. You know, like you old heads did back in the day." He raised his pistols a little higher. "Or we can take yo' punk-ass right here and right now. You ain't got enough bullets to hit everybody, but we got enough to turn yo' punk-ass into smothered pork chops."

I stepped up a stair. "Bitch, you ain't said nothin'. What's happening? Let's put these guns down and I'ma whoop you like I used to whoop yo' soft-ass daddy." I had a death wish and I knew it, but there was no way I was going to let this street punk talk that shit to me. I didn't like his father, and I damn sure didn't like him. I knew there was no way he could stand toe-to-toe with me and prevail. I was down for whatever.

Kazi laughed and nodded his head. "Nigga, let's get it." He lowered his gun and turned his back on me. I had a vision of emptying my clip into his ass, and the only thing that stopped me was hearing the downstairs door open, followed by a bunch of footsteps taking the stairs. I looked down to see the face of Hunter and two members from his all-beefy white boys, in all black, with their guns raised. He must've tracked me by the chip in my phone.

"Freeze, bastards, and drop your weapons!" he hollered before the ones that stood behind Kazi took off running up the stairs.

Kazi mugged me with hatred and acted as if he wasn't impressed. "My offer still stands. We can take this shit to the roof and get it in. Neither mine nor your homeboys got shit to do wit' this."

The next thing I knew I was removing my police-issued jacket and handing it over to Hunter as the rain pounded into my face and drenched my clothes. Looking about twenty feet across from me, Kazi had already taken his shirt off, and two of his Crip homies stood behind him with scowls on their faces. He mugged me with hatred as the lightning flashed across the sky.

Jelissa

I shrugged my shoulders and rolled my head around on my neck, then put up my guards and made my way over to him. He didn't actually move until I was within arm's reach. That's when he swung out with all of his might, trying to knock me out with one punch, yet only catching me in the neck. *Bam!*

"Bitch-ass nigga!"

I stumbled to my left as the pain shot all the way around to my spine, freezing me in place for a moment. Before I could allow that blow to sink in, he rushed me at full speed, picked me up, and slammed me to the pavement, causing my head to slam backward with a loud crack. I felt dizzy almost immediately.

"Get yo' punk-ass up, nigga! Get up! I knew you was soft. I knew you wasn't 'bout that life!" He stood over me and raised his Timbs, preparing to stomp me in the ribs when I rolled to my side and swept his legs from under him with a ground roundhouse. Lightning flashed across the sky again, the wind picked up, and rain drenching my clothes. They were matted to me and felt heavy, along with my bulletproof vest. I hopped to my feet from my back and held up my guards as he did the same.

He nodded his head. "Aw, you wanna do that police shit, huh? A'ight, nigga. Come on!"

He rushed me again, this time throwing so many blows at one time I couldn't block them all. He caught me in the jaw, then the nose, then the earlobe, and the next thing I knew he had his hands wrapped around my waist and was lifting me in the air before falling backward, slamming me on my shoulder blades. *Whom!* Then he hopped back up and shook up with one of his crewmembers.

"I told you, cuz. I told you Shotgun was a bitch. That nigga ain't got no hands, kid, word is bond." He shook up with the second dude. They hugged and said something to each other I couldn't make out.

I felt like I had been paralyzed. I could barely move a muscle, and every time I tried to it hurt like hell. Thunder roared loudly overhead. The rain felt like hail coming from the sky. I slid my hand under my waistband and grabbed the .380 pistol, cocking it with my back to Kazi and his crew. I made eyes with Hunter. He clearly saw what I was doing and simply nodded his head and looked over at the gangbangers.

Kazi slowly made his way over to me as a big bolt of lightning flashed across the sky, illuminated it. "Get yo' bitch-ass up, Shotgun. You gon' pay for what you did to my mother, fuck-nigga! And my father!"

"Yo, stomp him out, kid. Word is bond. Stomp his ass in the ground, Kazi! Fuck that pig!" said his heavyset homie with rain beating off his Yankees hat.

Kazi turned to me and frowned, then ran over and raised his Timberland boot to stomp me into the ground, I imagined. But as soon as he raised his foot, I let his ass have it nine times. *Boom. Boom. Boom.* The first bullet slammed into his stomach, knocking him backward. He hollered out in pain. The next bullets tore at his midsection before he fell to the ground on his knees, crawling across the pavement with blood pouring from him. "You coward-ass nigga." Then he fell on his face, lifeless.

The next thing I knew Hunter and his crew were letting off multiple slugz at Kazi's members. They seemed to catch them from every which way. Every time they squeezed their triggers, it would illuminate the night sky.

Hunter came over and knelt beside Kazi after taking what I assumed to be a dirty pistol off his waist, wrapping the kid's hand around it, raising his arm skyward and shooting in the air twice before placing his arm back down. His crew did the same thing to Kazi's men.

I held my ribs and limped over beside Hunter. "I owe you one. I know this, and I won't forget it. You got my word on that."

Hunter pulled me into his embrace and gave me a half hug. "Funny you should say that, because I have a little bit of

Jelissa

business that I need your help with. What do you know about a Blood named Ramsey?"

***

Rome

"Chucky, you stop that shit right now, and don't you do it. Don't worry, we'll get 'em back. He won't get away wit' this, trust me," Randy hollered, and lightning struck a tree about fifteen yards away from us. It sounded like one of them had let off their shotgun.

Tia kicked opened the backdoor, and I slowly moved backward into the truck, taking Randy right along with me. His wet hair smelled like a dog's ass, I imagined. "Look, man, when we get to the edge of the road I'ma let you out. I ain't tryna kidnap you. But I can't let y'all kill me and her out here. It ain't nothin' personal."

Chucky pointed the shotgun into the truck, once again right against my ear. "Let me kill 'im, Randy. We can't let him take you to the ghetto. Those niggas a kill you down there."

"Randy, tell him to get that gun off me or we both gon' die." I just knew that white boy was finna kill me. I kept on imagining him pulling the trigger and knocking my brains all over the interior of my truck. I stuffed the barrel to Randy's temple. "Tell 'im to back off, Randy. Now! Tia, pull off!"

She threw the car in reverse and began to slowly back it out of the parking spot.

"It's okay, Chucky. He's gonna let me go. We'll get 'im later, you can bet yo' bippy."

"But, Randy —" were the last words I heard before Tia stepped on the gas, sending the truck backward with mud shooting in the air. She floored it all the way backward until our tires hit the road, then she threw the truck into drive and stepped on the gas, sending gravel in the air. I waited until we were about a mile down before I opened the door and pushed his big ass out of it.

Me and Tia checked into a motel about an hour later. I paced back and forth while she sat on the bed with her face in her hands. I'd already sent Ramsey a text letting him know I needed to speak with him, and it was urgent.

Tia rubbed her face wit' her hands and shook her head from side to side. "Them white boys could have killed us back there. What the fuck do Ramsey got us walking into?" she said, looking up at me. She seemed bewildered and shaken up, and I couldn't blame her one bit because I was, too.

She stood up and walked in front of me, stopping me in my tracks before wrapping her arms around me. "I swear to God I thought I was gone tonight. I saw them white boys killing you, and that crushed my soul. I can't handle somethin' happening to you, Sharome. I'd lose my fucking mind. I swear I would." She lay her head on my wet chest and snuggled her face into me.

I hugged her and rubbed her back. "We good. Don't trip, ma. Ramsey gon' help us figure all this shit out. He got to. Let's just try our best to get some type of rest. Then in the morning we can take our ass home and regroup as much as we can." I leaned down and kissed her on the forehead, and she held me tighter wit' her eyes closed.

In all honesty, even though I was missing Leesee like crazy and my every other thought was of her, I couldn't deny the fact I was casually developing feelings for Tia, as much as I hated to admit that. I knew that was real doggish of me, and it wasn't right, but it was like her and I were constantly going through one thing after the next together and overcoming things side-by-side. And I didn't care who a nigga was, if he had somebody who went through trials and multiple tribulations with him and the two of them emerged from them stronger and stronger, it was nearly impossible to not fall for that one. Especially if the person was of the opposite sex.

At the same time, all me and Leesee seemed to do half the time was argue and walk on eggshells around one another, whereas Tia was my escape from all of those discomforts. So yeah, she had me feeling some type of way, and as a man I had to just keep that one hunnit wit' myself.

She took a step backward out of my embrace and looked up at me with her pretty brown eyes. "Sharome, I know you might not be thinking about no shit like this, but can you lay me down and make love to me, just for a little while? I just need to be with you one last time, then I promise on my soul I will never come at you again. From here on out we can just be cool, even though that's going to be hard for me. But I'm asking. Please?"

She placed both of her hands on my chest and rubbed over it, looking me in my gray eyes while biting on her bottom lip. I don't know why when females did that it turned me on so much, but it was one of my weaknesses, especially when she did it. I think I loved the complexion of her skin a lot, too, so her whole li'l setup was getting the better of me.

I shook my head. "Man, ma, I can't keep doin' yo' cousin like that. I'm starting to feel real low and everything, even though you are tempting as hell. That and you go me feeling some type of way about you because you been so one hunnit. But I gotta be a man and end what we been doing because it ain't fair to her. I love that girl, man, and I gotta be the best man I possibly can be for her. You understand that?" I asked, watching the tears roll down her cheeks. I wiped them away with my fingers and hugged her to me.

She tried to shake her head, but her face was planted against my chest. "But it's not fair, Sharome, because I love you, too. And I deserve a man like you." She sniffed loudly, her voice breaking up with every other word. "All my life all men have ever done is take advantage of me. They've beat me, raped me, and tried to kill me so many times I've lost count.

134

No man has ever cared about me, including my father, so I thought all men were dogs. And then you came along, and I see how good you treat my cousin. I've witnessed how you treat her like a real, live queen. You cater to her, and you'll do anything in this world for her, and I just never thought it was possible. I didn't think you men could feel that way about us, and now that I do, I want that for myself. I want you for myself, but since I can't be selfish then I'm willing to share you with her, and she never has to know." She looked up at me. "Sharome, please, just give me a chance. I'll never try to break you guys up. I'll always give you the best advice when it comes to you all's relationship. I'm not looking for anyone to get hurt, I just want to share your love. Like SZA, I'll be happy if you give me the weekends."

More tears sailed down her cheeks, and seeing them made me feel a bit emotional, because besides Leesee, no one had ever loved me enough to cry over me. Not even my own mother, who I felt hadn't really loved me at all. So, seeing those tears of need for me was causing me to become weaker for her.

I wiped her tears away and looked onto her beautiful face that was without makeup. Light freckles decorated her dark cheeks. There were light hairs on the top of her upper lip, barely visible, and I found them sexy. I didn't understand what was going on with me.

I leaned my head all the way down and kissed her thick lips, sucking them into my mouth. She moaned and took a deep breath, opened her mouth wider, then sucked my lips into her mouth. Our noses were pressed up against each other's. Her arms tightened around the small of my back, pulling me closer.

"Unh! I need you, Sharome. Please, just one more time."

She licked my lips, sucked the bottom one into her mouth, and ran her tongue across it. She reached down and started to unbuckle my pants. I took a deep breath and exhaled as I felt her hands slide into my boxers. They were still damp from the rain. Her hot hand squeezed my penis, then she ran her thumb back and forth across my helmet. That made me jerk, and I began to rise while I groaned into her mouth.

"Damn, Tia, you finna make me do this shit again. Damn. Why you gotta be so fuckin' sexy?" I reached down and cupped her ass, massaging it like dough, feelin' its weight and softness. She moaned louder as I trailed my hands all the way under her cheeks and felt the heat of her crease.

She took her hand out of my boxers, took a step back, and pulled her Prada jeans to the floor, along with her red lace boyshort panties, kicking them to the side. Then she walked to the bed and put one of her small feet up on it, taking her hand and separating her sex lips. "Sharome, get over here and eat this pussy, now!" she ordered with a frown on her face.

I watched her slide two fingers into herself, pull them out, the suck them into her own mouth, and I thought it was the hottest thing in the world. I loved the way pussy tasted, so for a woman to love the taste of herself, Aw, man. It just did something to me.

I walked over and fell to my knees in front of her, grabbing her ass with both of my hands, and forcing my face into her mound, eating it hungrily, sucking and licking up and down and in between her sex lips, rubbing my nose back and forth across her clitoris.

"Un, un, un! Yes, yes, eat this pussy, Sharome. Ooh, ah, just like that, baby. Just let me be yo' side. Just let me be yo' side piece. I won't ever say nothin'. Ooh, I promise! Unh! Shit!" she hollered and got to humping into my face at full speed while I held that big-ass booty.

Her kitty's scent wafted up my nose. I loved it. It had a tinge of sweat to it as well, but it only added to my arousal. In my opinion there was nothin' like the natural scent of a woman.

I picked her ass up by her hips and slammed her to the bed, pushed her knees to her chest, and sucked her kitty like I was trying to pull something out of it. My chin was all in her ass crack, and I kept on going, sucking and pulling on her clit until she was shaking and begging me to fuck her.

"Ah, ah. Ooh. I'm cumming, Sharome! Ooh! Sharome! I'm cumming, Daddy! Uh!" she hollered, trying her best to sit up, but I was holding onto the back of her knees, forcing them to her chest while I attacked her kitty.

The next thing I knew she was lying on her side with me behind her. I had a handful of her hair and her right thigh over my forearm, pounding that pussy out with all of my might. Every time I slammed forward into her, her thick ass cheeks would jiggle, along with her thighs. The heat from her womb sucked at my pole, along with the walls. She seemed to have muscle control down there, and it was driving me crazy, making my toes curl.

I bit into her neck and sucked loudly, tasting her skin as I pumped back and forth with her juices dripping off my balls. "Uh, uh, uh, uh. Give me this pussy, Tia. Give me this shit! Uh, this shit so good. It's so good!" I growled, speeding up the pace with my pubic hairs slapping into her ass. I lifted her leg further upward and got to gritting my teeth as I drove into her with a vengeance.

"Cum in me, Sharome. Uh! Cum in my pussy, Daddy! It's okay! Please, Daddy, it's okay! Uh!" She humped back into me again and again. That big booty did something to me. It felt like she was milking me with her walls.

The next thing I knew I felt my orgasm coming from all over my body. First my vision got blurry, then my arms tensed up, along with my legs. My balls started to vibrate, and then they disappeared into my stomach. Then I was cumming in large globs into her hot pussy. "Argh, shit!" I groaned with my body jerking like crazy.

"Un, un, un, un, un!" she screamed, bouncing that big ass back into me, sucking at my pipe like her kitty was giving me head. "I'm cumming, Sharome. Ooh, I'm cumming again. Yes, yes, yes!" She slammed back into me with all of her

Jelissa

might, reached behind her and grabbed my waist, forcing me to go as deep into her as I could.

Once there, I stayed still while my piece jerked inside her, releasing its joy. "Damn, Tia, you gon' get a muthafucka in trouble," I gasped, out of breath and rubbing all over that big, soft ass. I slid my finger into her crack and everything.

She laughed. "Shit, you ain't gon' be the only one. Mm, that dick so good, though, Sharome. You got me hooked on all that meat." She turned all the way on her side and placed her ass up against my front, turned so our lips could meet, and sucked on my lips, licking them with her tongue.

I kept right on rubbing that booty. I still couldn't believe how strapped she was and that she had cried for me. I grabbed her cheeks and squeezed them.

She broke our kiss and rubbed her nose into mine before placing her back to my chest. "Sharome, you know by me being yo' side chick it come wit' a bunch of benefits, right?"

She moved her ass all around in my lap. I felt my dick getting hard again. Her heat and the scent of her was driving me nuts. "Oh yeah? What kind of benefits?" I sucked on the back of her neck, then licked along her spine.

She shuddered. "Well, for one, I'm about to let you fuck me right in here, because I see you obsessed with all of this project booty." She smacked herself on the ass, reached backward, and grabbed my dick. "What you think about that?"

I was so hard all I could do was grab her hair and pull her up until she was on all fours with me behind her.

Chapter 14

Shotgun

I took the cool rag and wiped the sweat away from my forehead knocking on Simone's door again. The weather in Newark was crazy. One minute it was hot, then the next it was cold. Four hours prior it had been raining like crazy, and now here it was, nine o'clock in the morning, and the sun was shining bright in the sky. The humidity was through the roof, and I could barely breathe because the air was so thick. I wiped my face again and beat on the door.

It opened just as I was about to start kicking on that muthafucka. As soon as it did, Simone appeared. Cool air rushed into my face from her home. It felt like relief. I stepped in past her and closed my eyes with my tongue out, loving the feel of the cold inside.

She slammed the door and locked it, then walked in front of me, poking me in the chest with her forefinger three times. "You gon' fix this shit, Shotgun, or I swear we gon' have a problem. Now, I respect you, and I know you crazy and all that good shit, but what this nigga just did to me I can't accept, and it's yo' fault," she said with her face in a glare.

I bumped her out of my way, reached down, and smacked her on that jiggly booty that was encased in a tight Alexander Wang dress. "Go get me some cold lemonade, then come in here and tell me what the fuck you talkin' about. Treat the god like a king first, though, nah mean?" I said, flopping down on the couch and setting my phone on her glass table.

I was expecting a call from Hunter. He wanted me to knock off some low-level Jamaican dealers out in D.C. with him later on that night. He said he'd call me with the specifics. We were looking to get away with fifty gees and few kilos of dope. It was petty money to me, but I owed him a favor after

Jelissa

he helped me knock off Kazi and his Crip buddies. One hand washed the other.

Simone looked me over for a long time with her leg extended and her right hand on her big hip. She was about forty-somethin' years old but had the body of a goddess and the face to match. I just liked my women a whole lot younger, if you get my drift.

"You know what, Shotgun? I'ma go get you this lemonade, but you gon' start respecting me. I ain't playing, neither. I'm ti'ed of this shit. Muthafucka come in my house, talking any ol' way to me," She mumbled all the way down the hallway toward the kitchen.

I laughed and sat back with my hands behind my head, as comfortable as I wanted to be. I closed my eyes and saw Ramsey's face. Was he fucking Leesee, too, I wondered. Had they turned my baby girl out to the mob like they did other hoez? I shook my head and thought back to a time when my Shotgun Posse did those type of things to Sharome's mother and a few other females in our circle. Back then, shit, even Simone had gotten a taste of the old choo-choo train of the Posse. Damn, I hoped Leesee was still as pure as she was the day I lost her.

Simone came back into the living room and sat down a coaster, then a white, folded cloth. Then she placed a big, clear glass pitcher of lemonade on top of the cloth and the empty glass onto the coaster before pouring me a glass full. Big ice cubes fell into the glass, and I smiled at that.

"A'ight, Shotgun, here you go. Now hear me out."

She stood in front of me, looking down with a serious look. I grabbed the glass and shook it around, allowing the ice cubes to cool my drink before I took a long swallow. Mm, nice and sweet, just like I liked it. "What can I do for you, Simone?"

"That son of a bitch you brought over here came back yesterday and took those girls away, threw my money back in my face, saying 'all or nothin'.'" She slammed her fist into her

140

hand. "Now, you know I don't play that shit, and I would have never allowed for that to happen, but as I opened the door, he had three men run into my house with guns and masks all over their faces. I couldn't do shit because he had the jump on me. I watched him file them girls into a U-Haul truck. Then he dropped the duffle bag containing the forty thousand dollars at my feet and said 'all or nothin', bitch' before walking out of my house like he was a straight-up gangsta. Blew my wig back because I know how you get down. I know you'd never let nobody do me like that, but he did, and now I don't know what to do. I got tricks already lined up for those girls, coming all the way from Maine just to spend a few nights with them at five grand a night for three nights. Four times five is twenty, twenty times three is sixty gees. I can't afford to lose that kind of dough." She reached on the side of the couch and picked up a Louis Vuitton Birkin bag and set it at my feet. "That's the forty he gave me back. It's all yours. All I want is my girls," she said, looking me over.

I raised my right eyebrow and grabbed the money, looking inside of it and thumbing through the cash. "You talking about Savan, right? That pretty nigga I fuck with on the sex trafficking along the coast?"

She nodded and reached into her bra, handing me a card. "Yeah, that's him, and this is his address. Don't ask me how I got it, 'cause I don't reveal my sources. You just handle his ass, Shotgun Posse-style, Shotgun, and let me thank you in advance."

She sat beside me, I assumed to give me a hug. I bounced up and mugged the shit out of her. "Nah, we ain't gon' do all that, but I got you, though. I'ma go holler at this nigga right now."

***

Leesee

It felt like the walls were closing in on me as I stood in the basement, looking over the ten Spanish girls who were bound by duct tape. Savan came up behind me and wrapped his arms around my waist, placing his chin into the crux of me neck. "I don't wanna keep shit from you no more, Leesee. This is a part of me. I traffic these girls all over the east coast, but it's not as bad as you think."

He kissed my neck, and the feel of it repulsed me. I jerked out of him embrace. "Not as bad as I think. I think you got a bunch of little girls in your basement, tied up. This doesn't look right, Savan. I gotta get out of here." I shook my head and felt like I wanted to scream at the top of my lungs. I felt sick because I was really startin', to fall for his ass. I couldn't believe I'd betrayed Sharome for some kind of pervert kidnapper. I felt dumb as a box of rocks, and extremely guilty.

I made my way to the stairs when he grabbed me by my arm and yanked me backward to him. "Ah! Savan! Let me go. You're hurting my arm," I hollered in pain.

He picked me up and slammed me against the brick wall, placing his hand around my neck. "If you just listen to me instead of being so fucking stubborn!" he said through clenched teeth.

I looked over his shoulder and saw all of the girls huddled around each other. Their murmurings tugged at my heart strings. They looked afraid, and that made me feel sorry for them. I wondered how much they'd went through. What types of things had he already done to them? Were their parents looking for them? They were probably out of their minds with grief and worry over their little girls. I just couldn't believe I didn't see any of those traits in him. I felt honesty sick to my stomach.

"Savan, you need to let me go and tell me what's going on without putting your hands on me. I understand you're angry right now because you were found out, but you can't take this out on me. That's not fair," I said as calmly as I possibly could.

142

Love Me Even When It Hurts 2

He held me more firmly to the wall, looking into my face with his nose scrunched. He held me that way for a long time without saying a word. Then he simply let me go, pushing me a little.

"Look, you need to hear me out before you try to up and leave. You have to understand what this is all about before you judge me."

I straightened the button-up shirt he gave me after he'd ripped mine off of me. I rolled my shoulders and took a deep breath. "Go ahead. I'm listening."

Even though I was going to give him the place to speak, there was nothin' he was going to say that would change my mind about how I now felt about him. Looking at those girls caused me to wake all the way up. I felt horrible for them and for my choices as a woman. Sharome's face popped into my mind. He'd been so good to me, loved me like no other person ever had, and here I was cheating on him and finding out the man I'd been cheating with was nothing more than a sex trafficker of little girls. I deserved everything that was happening to me. I was such a fool, and my own worst enemy. I hated me so much.

Savan pointed at the little girls. "Those little girls were starving back in their homeland. Nobody gave a fuck about them, and had they not been sold to me, they would have more than likely been killed by a member of their own family because their mouths were too much to feed. You see, baby, at least here in America, under my care, they'll get three meals a day, clothes on their backs, and never have to worry about dying a horrible death. They can have their slice of the American dream, just like you and I. So, in a sense, I'm rescuing them from their torment."

I squinted my eyes and looked at him like he was a damn fool. "What do you do with them, mister hero? And be honest, because if you say anything other than 'make sure they are placed with loving families that won't hurt them' worse than you and their parents already have, you need to go to hell, you

143

sick son of a bitch!" I pushed him with all of my might and made a run for the stairs, taking them two at a time.

He flew backward into the water heater, then bounced back and started to come after me. "Leesee, get your little ass back here, bitch! You don't understand!"

I could hear his loud footsteps running up the flight. I got to the top and busted through the door with all of my might, falling on my chest in the kitchen and looking over my shoulder for him. Then I scrambled and got up in a frenzy, running toward the front door after grabbing my keys and purse off the table beside the couch.

He ran out of the basement, turned around, and slammed the door before pursuing me once again. "Leesee! Baby, please don't go! I need you, bitch! Can't you understand that?" he hollered at the top of his lungs.

I fumbled with the locks until I was able to swing the door open. The bright sun attacked me immediately, nearly blinding me. I ran outside and fell down the steps on my ass, not caring, not feeling any pain. I was in flight mode, trying my best to escape this demon of a man. I looked over my shoulder just as he appeared in the doorway. He ran down the stairs and jumped from the last two of them.

"Leesee. Baby, please! Don't do this! You don't understand!"

I jumped in my car, started the ignition, and pulled away from the curb. I looked in my rearview mirror and saw him getting into his Benz before storming away from the curb as well.

***

Rome

Tia straddled me, leaned down, and kissed my lips. "Good morning, baby. How did you sleep?"

Love Me Even When It Hurts 2

She as smiling. Her breasts jiggled just a little bit, both chocolate nipples enticing me. I pulled her all the way down and sucked the right one into my mouth, pulling on it a little with my teeth.

She shivered and arched her back. "Mm."

I gripped that ass and flipped her to her back, got between her legs, and looked down on her. "Yo, word is bond, no matter what me and Leesee got going on, I'm gon' always be there for you because you deserve that type of love ain't neither one of us ever had before. I heard everything you said last night, and I know you need me. But the thing is, I need you, too. So never feel like you no side nothin'. Wit' me and you it's bigger than that. You understand that?" I asked, rubbing the hairs of her eyebrows. There was nothin' like a beautiful black woman. Her skin alone made me feel obligated to go hard for her, regardless of our circumstances and her relation to A'Leeseea.

She sucked on her bottom lip and nodded her head. "Yeah, I do, and that makes me happy." She reached up and pulled me down, sucking all over my lips like she usually did, reaching between us and putting my dick inside her kat. I humped forward, going deep. "Mm!" she moaned, opening her legs wider.

My phone started to vibrate, and before could really get going and beating her walls loose, I reached over and picked it up. I looked at the face.

It was a text from Leesee that simply read, *"Help me!"*

I pulled my dick out of Tia. I tried to call A'Leeseea's phone back to back but received no answer. I sat the phone on the night table and began getting dressed.

Tia crawled across the bed wit' her ass in the air, titties jiggling on her perfect frame. "What's the matter, baby?" She jumped up, her sex lips peeking from between her thighs.

I slid my damp shirt over my head. "I just got a crazy text from Leesee. She saying she need help, but when I hit her phone, she ain't pickin' up. Something ain't right, and I'm

145

worried out of my mind. I gotta get home to her. You coming?"

She picked up her panties and slid them up her thick thighs, wiggling into them. "Hell yeah. I got yo' back, and hers, too. Let's find out what's goin' on." She ran over to me and kissed my lips hard, sucking on them. "Thank you for caring about me, too. That means more to me than you'll ever know. I really mean that, Sharome."

I looked down into her eyes and nodded. In that moment I really didn't have the words. Though I felt some type of way about her, I couldn't get Leesee off my mind. I had to get to my baby.

Chapter 15

Leesee

I slammed on the brakes, turned the car off, and took the key out of the ignition. I opened the driver's side door, ran out of it and up the stairs to my house just as I heard a car slam on its brakes with a loud screech. The sun shone down into my face, nearly blinding me. My vision was able to focus enough to allow me to see Savan jumping out of his Benz, running around his car and toward me at full speed. My eyes grew wide before I turned to the door, slid my key into the lock, and almost forgot how to do it. I felt like I was becoming dizzy as I heard the sound of his boots on the pavement.

"Leesee! Baby, wait a minute. Let me just talk to you for a second, please!" he hollered, rushing up the stairs.

I struggled with the key, and as soon as I turned it the right way and got the door open, Savan appeared behind me. "Ah!" I screamed as he grabbed a handful of my hair and forced me into the house, throwing me to the floor aggressively.

"Now, I said I need to talk to you, little girl! Why are you runnin' away from me?" he boomed with his eyes wide open. He looked like he was hopped up on drugs. Sweat poured down the sides of his face. His shirt was stuck to him, and he kept on clenching and unclenching his hands as if he was ready to explode.

I started to move backward on the floor to get away from him, looking up and not recognizing the monster that stood over me. "Savan, please leave me alone! Get out of my house. It's over between us," I whimpered scooting backward on my butt away from him. I looked all around for the closest weapon I could find, and in that moment that best thing I could find was a lamp. Unfortunately for me, it was closer to him than it was to me. In order for me to have gotten to it, I would have had to go through him, and I knew I didn't stand a chance. He was nearly six feet of solid muscle. I started to panic.

He continued to walk toward me with his eyes wide. "You ain't leaving me, Leesee. You know way too much. I won't allow you to be my downfall. So, it's either you going to come back and be with me, or I'm going to kill you right here and right now. Those are your only choices. So, what is it gonna be?" he hollered at the top of his lungs.

I shook my head and continued to scoot backward. "Savan, get out of here. I don't want to be with you. Why don't you just leave me the hell alone? I don't care about what you do. I'm not going to say anything. I just wanna be alone!" I continued to scan the house for a weapon after crossing the lamp off my list. The humidity had crept inside, causing me to sweat like crazy. It dripped down my neck and into my cleavage, making it hard for me to breathe. I prayed my asthma didn't begin to act up. I was already scared out of my mind.

Savan's face turned into a snarl. "Leave you alone! Bitch, now you want me to leave you alone? What happened to you needing me, Leesee? What happened to you being thankful I was there to console you when your father died? Huh? Huh? Bitch!" He reached down and grabbed my ankle roughly, pulling me toward him before he straddled me, wrapped is hands around my neck, and started to squeeze. "This that shit you like, anyway, ain't it, bitch? Ain't this the reason you couldn't stay away, huh? Isn't it?"

He started to choke me so tight his nails were digging into my neck. The air to my windpipe was cut off, and it made my eyes feel as if they were bugged out of my head. I humped upward into him and tried to shake him off my body, but it was to no avail. The more I twisted and turned, the harder he choked me until I was sure this man was going to kill me.

Sharome's smiling face popped into my head. I saw myself running into his arms and him scooping me up, carrying me around the bedroom as if I was a little girl while

I lay my face in the crux of his neck. He always smelled so fresh and clean. His muscles bulging out of his shirt sleeves as always. The only man in my life who had ever loved me for me and treated me like a queen. I missed him so much.

Savan slapped me across the face with all of his might, splitting my lip, picked my head up, and slammed it backward into the floor. "If I can't have you, Leesee, then nobody can. Die, bitch! Die! I can't let you ruin me!" He leaned down and really applied his muscles to his choking.

The more I struggled to breathe, the easier it was for me to make peace with the fact this man was I going to kill me.

***

Shotgun

Err! Doom! My head jerked forward as the car slammed into me from behind, causing my airbags to deploy in a loud *thwomp!* My face crashed into the airbag before I opened my driver's door and rolled out onto the hot pavement with the sun shining bright above me. The humidity seemed to smother me. I felt a sharp pain in my ribs and was sure I had broken a few of them, though I didn't remember how.

I struggled to get to my feet when I felt something crash into my back with a loud thud. I fell to my stomach and scraped my chin on the concrete before I felt the attack on my back again.

Whom! "Bitch-ass nigga!" *Whom!*

The weapon came down on my back again, and this time I hollered out in pain and flipped over onto my back, looking up to see a dark-skinned face with a blue rag around its neck.

Whom! "You kilt my brother, you bitch-ass nigga! You kilt my brother for nothin'. Now you gon' pay!" He lifted the golf club all the way over his head, then brought it down at full speed, connecting with my shoulder.

Jelissa

He worked me over as the bystanders stood off in the distance, recorded what was taking place with their cellphones. I covered my head and curled into a ball with my ribs screaming bloody murder. I took one hit after the next. They were getting harder and harder, coming faster. I could hear my bones cracking and feel the pain shooting all over me.

"They gon' kill that man!" somebody yelled from afar.

I prayed they called the police. I clearly needed help. "Ah! I am a police officer! Somebody help me, please! There is a reward in it for you!" I yelled just as one of the bats came down hard onto me again, crashing into my shoulder blade and shattering it. I screamed like a bitch and tightened the ball I had my body in.

I knew if I stayed there like that, those dudes were going to kill me. It seemed like there was no end in sight to their abuse. They had me in the middle of Franklin Street in broad daylight, beating me as if I was Rodney King. I felt my heartbeat speed up. I had to make a move. I had to get out of that circle before they murdered me in cold blood.

"Yo, pull his arms from his face, kid, so I can bash his mug in. Hurry up, son!" one of them said.

The abuse stopped for a second, and I felt them reaching for my wrists and trying to pull me out of the ball. I knew it was now or never, and in one spurt I shot up and ran as fast as I could out of their crowd and down the street, right through the bystanders who had refused to help me in any way.

"Yo, get his ass, kid. Don't let that nigga get away! Word is bond, he killed my brother, cuz, and that nigga Kazi!"

With every step I took I felt like I was about to pass out from the pain they had inflicted upon me. My ribs were killing me. It made it hard to breathe, and my vision was more than hazy, but I kept on going, glancing over my shoulder to see about six dudes chasing me and gaining ground.

I hit the corner, still looking over my shoulder, and bumped right into a heavyset, dark-skinned sista who was pushing a stroller, falling backward right on my ass. She flew over the stroller and landed on her back. "Hey, what the fuck is your problem?" she yelled just as her baby began to scream at the top of its lungs.

With sweat pouring down my face and my heart feeling like it was about to explode in my chest, I rushed to pull my left pant leg up as the gangbangers got closer and closer to me with their baseball bats and golf clubs. They were closing the distance between us fast. I leaned forward with my ribs throbbing, grabbed the .9 millimeter out of my ankle holster, cocked it, and began shooting just as the sista decided to jump up and into my line of fire.

***

Rome

I pushed the pedal to the metal, taking the truck to its top speeds, flying past a white dude with a helmet on the expressway who had been weaving in and out of traffic. The way I was feeling, I would've had no problem hittin' his ass and continuing right on my way home. I felt it deep within my bones that Leesee was in serious trouble. So, I flew alongside a big, white semi-truck, then cut in front of it, storming like a maniac.

Tia pulled her seatbelt around her body. "Baby, you need to slow down. I'm not kidding. There is no way you're going to be able to rescue her if we're all dead and in the morgue. Jesus Christ!" she screamed as I nearly sideswiped a purple Neon because I needed to get in front of it.

I shook my head. "Yo, don't worry about what I'm doing. You just keep on hitting her phone. See if she picks up. What did Shante say when you called?" I asked, storming in front of the Neon. The driver, some young sista about my age, started to blow her horn over and over again, but I ignored her and punched the gas a little harder, swerving to the middle lane as my pistol fell off my lap and to the floor.

Tia looked like she was about to throw up. "Slow down, Sharome! I can't even think straight." She looked out at the road, then covered her eyes as I swerved left and just made it in front of a white dude driving an Excursion. He blew his horn, and in my rearview mirror I could see him pick his cellphone up and start dialing it while holding it against the steering wheel. I didn't give a fuck.

I switched lanes again and mugged Tia. "What she say, Tia?" I hollered louder than I meant to.

"Damn, why you get all angry with me? This isn't my fault, you know." Her voice sounded as if it was breaking up.

I felt bad for yelling at her. Ever since we'd let each other know how we felt about one another, she seemed as if she'd gotten more emotional. I had to remember that.

I swerved and flew two lanes over, preparing to get on the exit ramp, in the process nearly slamming into a black Jetta I was sure had seen better days. "Look, I'm sorry, Tia. I'm just freaking out a li'l bit. I ain't mean to come at you wrong, okay? I need you right now. We gotta be strong for each other. It's the only way." I reached over and put my hand on her thigh, squeezing like she'd always done for me.

She nodded her head and smiled, sucking or her bottom lip. "It's cool, baby. I understand but thank you for saying that." She sat forward in her seat and tried to get some slack from her seatbelt by pulling the top part away from her chest. When she saw it wouldn't give, she unclicked it altogether, leaned over to me, and attempted to kiss me on the lips. "Gimme a kiss, baby, so I can calm down."

I nodded and leaned over with the intention of kissing her soft lips when her eyes got big and she screamed at the top of her lungs. "Oh my God, baby, watch out!"

By the time I turned to look back at the road, it was too late.

To Be Continued…
Love Me Even When It Hurts 3
Coming Soon

Thank you sincerely to those who continue to rock with me. I'm new out here in these streets of the literary world, LOL.

Stay connected with me on either of my Facebook pages, Authoress Jelissa Shanté or Author Jelissa Shanté. Please feel free to join "Feenin' For Fiction Readers Group", as well as the Mental Health Matters Support Family Group. God bless.

Love Always,

Jelissa

Submission Guideline

Submit the first three chapters of your completed manuscript to ldpsubmissions@gmail.com, subject line: Your book's title. The manuscript must be in a .doc file and sent as an attachment. Document should be in Times New Roman, double spaced and in size 12 font. Also, provide your synopsis and full contact information. If sending multiple submissions, they must each be in a separate email.

Have a story but no way to send it electronically? You can still submit to LDP/Ca$h Presents. Send in the first three chapters, written or typed, of your completed manuscript to:

**LDP: Submissions Dept
Po Box 870494
Mesquite, Tx 75187**

DO NOT send original manuscript. Must be a duplicate.

Provide your synopsis and a cover letter containing your full contact information.

Thanks for considering LDP and Ca$h Presents.

Coming Soon from Lock Down Publications/Ca$h Presents

BOW DOWN TO MY GANGSTA

By **Ca$h**

TORN BETWEEN TWO

By **Coffee**

BLOOD STAINS OF A SHOTTA **III**

By **Jamaica**

STEADY MOBBIN **III**

By **Marcellus Allen**

BLOOD OF A BOSS **V**

By **Askari**

LOYAL TO THE GAME **IV**

LIFE OF SIN II

By **T.J. & Jelissa**

A DOPEBOY'S PRAYER **II**

By **Eddie "Wolf" Lee**

IF LOVING YOU IS WRONG… **III**

LOVE ME EVEN WHEN IT HURTS **III**

By **Jelissa**

TRUE SAVAGE **VII**

By **Chris Green**

BLAST FOR ME **III**

A BRONX TALE III

DUFFLE BAG CARTEL III

By **Ghost**

ADDICTIED TO THE DRAMA **III**

Love Me Even When It Hurts 2

By **Jamila Mathis**

LIPSTICK KILLAH **III**

Mimi

WHAT BAD BITCHES DO **III**

A HUSTLER'S DECEIT 3

KILL ZONE **II**

By **Aryanna**

THE COST OF LOYALTY **III**

By **Kweli**

SHE FELL IN LOVE WITH A REAL ONE **II**

By **Tamara Butler**

RENEGADE BOYS **III**

By **Meesha**

CORRUPTED BY A GANGSTA **IV**

By **Destiny Skai**

A GANGSTER'S CODE **III**

By **J-Blunt**

KING OF NEW YORK IV

RISE TO POWER III

By **T.J. Edwards**

GORILLAZ IN THE BAY III

De'Kari

THE STREETS ARE CALLING II

Duquie Wilson

KINGPIN KILLAZ IV

STREET KINGS 2

Hood Rich

STEADY MOBBIN' **III**

157

Marcellus Allen

SINS OF A HUSTLA II

ASAD

TRIGGADALE II

Elijah R. Freeman

MARRIED TO A BOSS II

By Destiny Skai & Chris Green

KINGS OF THE GAME II

Playa Ray

<u>**Available Now**</u>

<u>RESTRAINING ORDER **I & II**</u>

By **CA$H & Coffee**

<u>LOVE KNOWS NO BOUNDARIES **I II & III**</u>

By **Coffee**

<u>RAISED AS A GOON I, II, III & IV</u>

<u>BRED BY THE SLUMS I, II, III</u>

<u>BLAST FOR ME I & II</u>

<u>ROTTEN TO THE CORE I III</u>

<u>A BRONX TALE I, II</u>

<u>DUFFEL BAG CARTEL I II</u>

By **Ghost**

<u>LAY IT DOWN **I & II**</u>

<u>LAST OF A DYING BREED</u>

<u>BLOOD STAINS OF A SHOTTA I & II</u>

By **Jamaica**

<u>LOYAL TO THE GAME</u>

LOYAL TO THE GAME II

LOYAL TO THE GAME III

LIFE OF SIN

By **TJ & Jelissa**

BLOODY COMMAS I & II

SKI MASK CARTEL I II & III

KING OF NEW YORK I II,III

RISE TO POWER I II

By **T.J. Edwards**

IF LOVING HIM IS WRONG…I & II

LOVE ME EVEN WHEN IT HURTS I II

By **Jelissa**

WHEN THE STREETS CLAP BACK I & II III

By **Jibril Williams**

A DISTINGUISHED THUG STOLE MY HEART I II & III

LOVE SHOULDN'T HURT I II III

RENEGADE BOYS I & II

By **Meesha**

A GANGSTER'S CODE I &, II III

By J-Blunt

PUSH IT TO THE LIMIT

By **Bre' Hayes**

BLOOD OF A BOSS **I, II, III & IV**

By **Askari**

THE STREETS BLEED MURDER **I, II & III**

THE HEART OF A GANGSTA I II& III

By **Jerry Jackson**

CUM FOR ME

CUM FOR ME 2

CUM FOR ME 3

CUM FOR ME 4

An **LDP Erotica Collaboration**

BRIDE OF A HUSTLA **I II & II**

THE FETTI GIRLS **I, II& III**

CORRUPTED BY A GANGSTA I, II & III

By **Destiny Skai**

WHEN A GOOD GIRL GOES BAD

By **Adrienne**

THE COST OF LOYALTY

By Kweli

A GANGSTER'S REVENGE **I II III & IV**

THE BOSS MAN'S DAUGHTERS

THE BOSS MAN'S DAUGHTERS II

THE BOSSMAN'S DAUGHTERS III

THE BOSSMAN'S DAUGHTERS IV

THE BOSS MAN'S DAUGHTERS **V**

A SAVAGE LOVE **I & II**

BAE BELONGS TO ME

A HUSTLER'S DECEIT I, II, III

WHAT BAD BITCHES DO I, II

By **Aryanna**

A KINGPIN'S AMBITON

A KINGPIN'S AMBITION **II**

I MURDER FOR THE DOUGH

Love Me Even When It Hurts 2

By **Ambitious**

TRUE SAVAGE

TRUE SAVAGE II

TRUE SAVAGE **III**

TRUE SAVAGE **IV**

TRUE SAVAGE **V**

TRUE SAVAGE **VI**

By **Chris Green**

A DOPEBOY'S PRAYER

By **Eddie "Wolf" Lee**

THE KING CARTEL **I, II & III**

By **Frank Gresham**

THESE NIGGAS AIN'T LOYAL **I, II & III**

By **Nikki Tee**

GANGSTA SHYT **I II &III**

By **CATO**

THE ULTIMATE BETRAYAL

By **Phoenix**

BOSS'N UP **I , II & III**

By **Royal Nicole**

I LOVE YOU TO DEATH

By Destiny J

I RIDE FOR MY HITTA

I STILL RIDE FOR MY HITTA

By **Misty Holt**

LOVE & CHASIN' PAPER

By **Qay Crockett**

TO DIE IN VAIN

SINS OF A HUSTLA

By **ASAD**

BROOKLYN HUSTLAZ

By **Boogsy Morina**

BROOKLYN ON LOCK I & II

By **Sonovia**

GANGSTA CITY

By **Teddy Duke**

A DRUG KING AND HIS DIAMOND I & II III

A DOPEMAN'S RICHES

HER MAN, MINE'S TOO I, II

CASH MONEY HO'S

By **Nicole Goosby**

TRAPHOUSE KING **I II & III**

KINGPIN KILLAZ I II III

STREET KINGS

By **Hood Rich**

LIPSTICK KILLAH **I, II**

CRIME OF PASSION I & II

By **Mimi**

STEADY MOBBN' **I, II**

By **Marcellus Allen**

WHO SHOT YA **I, II**

Renta

GORILLAZ IN THE BAY **I II**

DE'KARI

TRIGGADALE

Elijah R. Freeman

Love Me Even When It Hurts 2

GOD BLESS THE TRAPPERS I, II, III

THESE SCANDALOUS STREETS I, II, III

FEAR MY GANGSTA I, II, III

THESE STREETS DON'T LOVE NOBODY I, II

BURY ME A G I, II, III, IV, V

A GANGSTA'S EMPIRE I, II, III

Tranay Adams

THE STREETS ARE CALLING

Duquie Wilson

MARRIED TO A BOSS...

By Destiny Skai & Chris Green

KINGS OF THE GAME II

Playa Ray

<u>BOOKS BY LDP'S CEO, CA$H</u>

<u>TRUST IN NO MAN</u>

<u>TRUST IN NO MAN 2</u>

<u>TRUST IN NO MAN 3</u>

<u>BONDED BY BLOOD</u>

<u>SHORTY GOT A THUG</u>

<u>THUGS CRY</u>

<u>THUGS CRY 2</u>

<u>THUGS CRY 3</u>

<u>TRUST NO BITCH</u>

<u>TRUST NO BITCH 2</u>

<u>TRUST NO BITCH 3</u>

<u>TIL MY CASKET DROPS</u>

<u>RESTRAINING ORDER</u>

<u>RESTRAINING ORDER 2</u>

<u>IN LOVE WITH A CONVICT</u>

<u>Coming Soon</u>

BONDED BY BLOOD 2

BOW DOWN TO MY GANGSTA

www.ingramcontent.com/pod-product-compliance
Lightning Source LLC
Chambersburg PA
CBHW070038260626
47159CB00005B/2076